THE ALTER

A DYSTOPIAN DARK ROMANCE NOVELLA

USA TODAY BESTSELLING AUTHOR

BRYNN FORD

The Alter

More from the Author

www.brynnford.com
brynnfordauthor@gmail.com

Playlist

Such a Whore (Stellular Remix) by JVLA
Bloody City by Sam Tinnesz
Boys Like U by ZAND
KILLING TIME by Jordan Fiction
Choke by Poppy
yes & no by XYLØ
Pretend by The Anix & Intrelock
Shameless by Camila Cabello
Play with Fire by Sam Tinnesz & Yacht Money
Afterlife by Hailee Steinfeld
Infinity by Jaymes Young
Tantrum by Ashnikko
VILLAIN by K/DA & Madison Beer & Kim Petras
E-GIRLS ARE RUINING MY LIFE
by CORPSE & Savage Ga$p
I Disagree by Poppy
HELLSLIDE by Siiickbrain
Venom by Icon For Hire
Serial Killer by Moncrieff & JUDGE
Black Sea by Natasha Blume
Crazy by Digital Daggers

CONTENT WARNING

This dark romance story involves many triggering elements which may be upsetting for some readers. A complete list of tropes and triggers can be found on the author's website.

www.brynnford.com/triggers

CHAPTER ONE
deviant little artist

LIFE IS FRAGILE outside the Tower. Out there—in the city—you live every minute like it's your last because it very well could be.

But that's not my life anymore.

I'm a deviant little artist here, an artist and an angel. Like a prodigy, I paint pleasure with my body, serving as an angel in this space we call Heaven. Each night I have an assignment—serve fantasies as an angel or deliver torture and death as a demon. It's all a part of the job, and the job is necessary for survival. I've learned to love the role for what it is and the security it offers me in this nightmare city ruled by the Savage Syndicate.

I've served as an alter for a little more than a month now, and though I have to do the dirty work to stay here in the Tower, the job is worth it for the safe haven it grants me. Here, I feel like I'm home, safe, free—at least, as free as I can be without being allowed to leave.

I don't want to leave anyway, and I sure as fuck wasn't free to live my life when I was out there. The city streets are painted red with blood, lives turned chaotic and violent for those who didn't make it out of the city before the Syndicate takeover. That was nearly a decade ago.

I was ten years old when the world changed for those of us trapped in the city. But the Tower is protected; it's safe for alters like me who serve. We're aptly named for the manner of our service, alternating between angel and demon play for our nightly assignments.

And no, I'm not so delusional that I would refer to myself with names like *angel* or *demon*, as if I view myself in such high regard. Leave that level of pretentious narcissism to the Deity, as he's referred—my employer—god of the Tower and by his own will, god of the alters. In fact, the man is so high on his own power that no one knows who he is. He's faceless, nameless, untouchable. I'd be lying to say the thought of a man like that doesn't get me a little hot.

Tonight, I serve as an angel by will of the almighty himself. Angels serve on the seventh floor of the Tower and tonight, I've been assigned the White Room—my *favorite* room. It's plush, luxurious, boasting a ridiculously ornate king-sized canopy bed, just floating in the center of the space. It may as well be floating on a cloud, sitting atop the furry white rug that lays beneath it.

I love fucking the winning players in this bed. The canopy is draped with sheer ivory curtains that softly droop around us to the ground. It makes me feel cocooned inside the softness of a cloud. And if I climb on top, I can look out over the headboard to the large picture window beyond.

And that's the best part.

The view of the city from this window is spectacular. Up here, from this side of the Tower, I can look out and almost forget the violence and chaos on the streets. I can pretend things are normal out there. I can pretend that one day, I'll leave the Tower, go for a stroll down the sidewalk without carrying a sheathed knife strapped to my thigh for protection.

I look out at that view now as I rock my hips in a sultry dance, fucking the winning player's barely hard, old man cock. The players don't always have nice faces or good bodies—or even decent dicks, for that matter—but I can get off on the way they want me. I like the attention I get as an angel. This player groans like he's never been fucked before, which seems highly unlikely given his age. It is likely, though, that he's never fucked anyone quite like me.

That's what gives me a rush.

I lift my hands to my purple hair, combing my fingers through at the scalp and pushing it up as I arch my back. I really put on the show, making him think that fucking him is a fantasy for me as much as it is for him. That's my job as an angel—fulfilling the winning player's fantasy.

This one didn't want anything fancy. I think he was just ecstatic to have won his bet and to have the pleasure of an angel's company. He asked for straight-up vanilla sex with me on top—boring as fuck. But I'll make him come, and I'll come, too, knowing he's never had a ride like this before, and probably never will again.

"One minute left," my keeper says from where he stands beside the door.

I sigh. There's no way I'm leaving this room until the player finishes, but my keeper will call the authority to drag us both out if we're not done when playtime is over. Time is tick, tick, ticking away. I flip my hair to one side and bend down over the old man, coming in close, but not so close that I block his view of my bouncing tits.

"Oh, you're gonna make me come, baby." I moan as I pick up the pace. "Come on, baby. Come inside me."

I literally can't fuck this guy any harder. It took the entire hour just to get him hard, and maybe that's why his fantasy was so boring—because it takes him so long to get it up. Maybe he can't get it up because he's so boring.

The chicken or the egg?

Seriously, what's wrong with this guy?

I'm rocking and moving so hard and so fast that it would be impossible for me not to come. He has all my carefully curated sexuality smothering him with pleasure, and he's still not there.

Maybe that's what he needs—my climax to trigger his.

I'm practically there anyway, so I let go. In seconds, I explode with a satisfying, albeit perfectly expected and ordinary, orgasm. Just like I'd hoped, that's the thing that tips him over the edge. He stutters through a groan with a look of surprise on his face. I wonder whether he's surprised that he could come at all, or surprised that I'm so good at this that it makes him shatter. Either way, I moan in time to his shaky, shocked-as-hell orgasm.

"Time's up," my keeper says, and I immediately move to climb off the bed.

"Nice work, old man," I tell the player as I bend to grab my white lace panties and bralette from the floor. "I wasn't sure if we were gonna make it there. Nothing like waiting until the last minute, huh?"

My keeper makes sure the old man stays away from me as I get dressed, a protective measure to ensure my safety—and to ensure the players don't take more than their winnings afford them. He got his hour with me, and that's all he'll get.

I pull on my panties—which hardly cover my ass cheeks—followed by the skimpy bralette. I slip my thigh-high stockinged feet into my white stiletto stripper heels and raise to my feet.

Before I can take a single step, the door unlocks from the outside and swings open without warning, startling me off-balance, and I fall back to sit on the edge of the bed.

"These fucking shoes," I mutter as my keeper walks toward the man in a black suit entering the room—he's one of the authority.

"She just finished, give her a minute," my keeper tells the authority and earns himself a fist slamming against his jaw.

"Well, fuck!" I shoot to my feet, placing my fists dramatically on my hips, jutting one out to the side. "What has gotten into you boys, huh? All this fighting over little old me?"

"The authority requests your presence."

"Right now? I haven't even had time to clean up."

"Come with me, please," the blond man in the black suit says, waving me forward with his hand.

This is unusual.

Interesting.

My pulse ticks, my heart pumping a little quicker.

"Fine," I say, walking around the bed. I stop briefly in front of the old man, who is sitting on the edge of the bed buckling his pants. I place my palms together in front of me and give him a little bow. "Pleasure to serve you, good sir. I hope you have an excellent evening."

"Tempest," my keeper calls after me, one hand on his presumably aching jaw as he follows the black suit out the door.

I've never been called in by the authority before, and my curiosity is piqued. I'm intrigued to know what's going on, but if I were thinking rationally, I could make a guess as to what this is about.

I hope it's not what I think it is.

Because if it is, I'm in big fucking trouble.

Two men from the authority usher me and my keeper down the hallway. The white-painted walls are adorned with gold-framed mirrors of various sizes, making the narrow space look bright with reflected light from the chandelier overhead.

At the end of the hallway, they shuffle us into the elevator, and one of them steps inside with us briefly, standing in front of the retinal scanner, which I don't think I've ever actually seen being used before. It's only needed to access certain floors that are off-limits to alters and their keepers.

I watch with a gaping mouth as a red light scans the man's eye and beeps its approval. He presses the button next to the number thirty on the panel, and it lights up. Then, he steps off the elevator and watches us as the metal doors slide shut.

The thirtieth floor...

I've never been on the thirtieth floor before—I don't know anyone who has. My fingers twitch against my upper thigh, drumming in time to my rapidly beating pulse over the bare skin exposed between my skimpy panties and thigh-high stockings.

I'm unusually aware of my lack of clothing. It's unusual

because I'm used to walking around the Tower scantily-clad. Mostly I wear lingerie or leather depending on my assignment for the night, just as all the other alters do. But this whole situation is bizarre.

I've never had an official meeting with the authority, not even to interview for my position as an alter. That was conducted in an empty room with a phantom voice over a loudspeaker. I saw no one, and I doubt I'll ever find out to whom that voice belonged.

I only ever see the authority when they bring struggling players to the Hellscape beneath the Tower—that's where we play demon. I suppose I did see them one other time, when they had to come to the twentieth floor—where the alters stay—to break up an altercation. That was a one-off because each alter has a keeper, and those men usually handle any squabbles or disagreements with ease. Other than that, they've managed to remain mostly elusive, and I've been okay with leaving them that way.

I glance sideways at my keeper. "Have you ever had to meet with the authority?"

His jaw is tense and his nostrils flare with the heavy breaths he takes. "No."

"Do you know anyone who has?"

"No." He pinches his eyes shut.

"Is this good or bad?"

His head snaps to look at me with wide eyes and a fearful gaze. "Shut the fuck up, Tempest. I don't know."

I press my lips together to stifle a laugh. I've never seen him so worked up, and it's a comical departure from his usual composure. "My, my, aren't we on edge tonight?"

He turns toward me. "What did you do?"

"Come again?"

"What the fuck did you do? Did you do something stupid to get in trouble? I need to know before we walk in there."

"I haven't done *anything*. I'm clueless. Maybe I'm just so amazing that they're calling me in for a promotion. You'll get to ride my coattails all the way to the top, asshole. Congratulations!" I clap, sarcasm ripe in my tone. "You're welcome."

I roll my eyes and flip my head as I turn away from him, focusing my attention on the electronic sign above the elevator doors that counts the numbers on the floors.

Twenty-eight, twenty-nine, thirty.

Ding.

I hold out my hand in a sweeping, dramatic gesture as the elevator doors part. "After you, good sir."

He shakes his head as he marches forward, muttering under his breath, "Fucking bitch."

Ouch.

That would really hurt if I gave a shit what he thought of me.

I follow him off the elevator and stop suddenly. This floor is a fucking black hole. I feel as though I've stepped off the elevator and landed in limbo. There are no hallways, no entries, no exits. Just the elevator behind me, black walls that surround me, and a single door straight ahead.

The dark walls form a square around us, locking us into this small space with only a single way of escape. I swallow hard, noting the rough wallpaper pasted on the walls, with its alternating stripes of gloss and matte black. The floorboards and crown molding are painted black, too, as is the ceiling.

It's ominous.

I can feel the way this space sucks the life out of me. It's silent and still. It would be pitch dark if it weren't for the single dim light hanging overhead. It's unnerving because the lack of everything doesn't feel good or bad—I don't feel any energy here at all. It's just a vacuum that sucks out emotion and makes me hyper-focused on sensation.

I can hear my heartbeat behind my ears. I'm suddenly aware of how dry my eyes feel, how sticky my thighs are from the aftermath of fucking, how forcefully the adrenaline whooshes through my veins.

Fascinating...

My keeper lifts a shaking hand to pound his fist on the single door in front of us, and then we wait.

Thirty seconds.

A full minute.

Then, a voice comes from a loudspeaker overhead. "Come inside. Don't plan on speaking unless spoken to."

I put the side of my hand against my forehead and give

a salute into the void, not knowing whether anyone can see us on a hidden camera. My keeper looks back at me with a severe expression, warning me with his eyes to cut the bullshit and behave.

Behave.

As if behaving ever mattered in saving a life in this city. I learned the hard way that it doesn't pay to follow the rules—not when your life is on the line, not when your families' lives hang in the balance. My brother might still be alive had I just broken the fucking rules the Syndicate made me think we were playing by—the only one playing by the rules was me. All that came of it was my brother's death and a bucket full of assault and trauma for me.

I only follow the rules here for my job because the Deity, who rules the Tower, offers protection from the Savage Syndicate and the brutal world they've crafted outside.

I don't get paid.

I don't have a life or friends or family outside of the Tower.

All I have is my life as an alter, and I'm thankful for it.

It's either this or death on the streets.

My keeper turns the knob and pushes the door open, and I'm practically jumping to see inside. I'm a little terrified, to be honest, because I don't exactly know what I'm walking into here. But this is an excited kind of terrified—my adrenal system doesn't understand the difference between anticipation and fear.

My keeper steps inside first, and I'm bouncing to follow behind him, but as soon as I cross the threshold, my shoulders droop in disappointment. There's nothing all that special here. It's an office—a massive, lovely office, but an office, nonetheless.

But then I see it.

Oh, my God!

I run across the space to look out the wide picture window, which spans the entire far wall from left to right, nearly from the floor to the ridiculously tall ceiling. It looks out over the nighttime city, and it's the same perfect view as the one from the White Room on the seventh floor, only it's just a little more spectacular.

"Oh, wow," I murmur, gazing out at the sparse city lights.

I have a memory of being a little girl, looking out at the same city, and seeing nothing but lights on every floor, in every window. Now, I could actually count the number of lights out there on my two hands, but those lights are beautiful all the same. They remind me that the world still turns, that I'm not dead, that I'm very much alive, and for the time-being, I'm well. My heart skips a beat and I bite down on my bottom lip.

"What the fuck are you doing?"

A chill shoots down my spine at the startling voice, and I spin to face it, only to step back immediately. My ass slams against the window. A man—a fucking *god*—stands inches in front of me, and I have to lift my head just to look up at his face.

Fuck, he's tall.

He's a giant slice of man towering above my five feet five inches—five feet eight inches in my heels.

He's beautiful.

He's something… otherworldly.

This man is the fucking black hole I felt in the dark space outside this office.

It's him.

He's the gravity that sucks my energy from me, draining my emotions, stealing them, and owning them for himself.

"Holy fucking hell," I say softly, and I instantly know I should've kept my big mouth shut.

This beast of a man, with his square jaw, dark scruffy beard, deep dark eyes, and dark brown *shaggy-wavy-fuck-me* hair reaches out to snatch me by the throat without so much as a twitch in his expressionless face.

He clutches me in his firm grip and tugs me away from the window. He spins me, marches me toward the single wooden desk floating just beyond the window, and shoves me down, face-first.

CHAPTER TWO
blood and life and death

I PUT MY hands out to catch myself as he bends me over the edge of the desk, but the wind is knocked out of my lungs all the same. I gasp for a breath as I feel him shift behind me, press against me, fold over me.

"It's a pleasure to make your acquaintance, Tempest." His voice is a growling whisper that sends a shiver down my spine.

I swallow, trying to force down my natural sarcasm, but it's no use. It's always worse when I'm feeling defensive. "No, no, the pleasure is all mine. How can I help you today?"

He grasps my hair at the base of my neck, fisting it into a ponytail. With a sharp tug, he lifts me from the desk, just enough so my breasts rise from the surface and I'm forced to arch my back at an angle that's almost painful—not that I mind a little pain…

"It's gonna be best for you if you shut your fucking mouth. You're on thin ice right now."

"How exactly did I get on the ice? I'm not much for skating."

He chuckles darkly. "Are you fucking dumb?"

"I might be. Never did finish school, what with the city being violently taken over and all. But you seem to have done pretty well for yourself. Maybe you can teach me a thing or two."

With a flick of his wrist, he tosses me aside and I tumble—rather ungracefully—to the floor, losing one of my shoes in the process. I roll onto my hands and knees so I can stand back up, but his heavy combat boot slams down in the center of my back, slamming me flat to the floor. I hit with an *oomph* as air rushes heavily from my lungs. I try to push up with my hands, but he holds me firmly in place. There's an odd little flutter in my belly that I don't quite understand.

"You're in trouble, little girl."

Shit.

I feign surprise. "What? I'm *shocked*. What have I done?"

He removes his foot from my back. "Get on your knees."

Inexplicably, I do as I'm told. I sit back on my heels and lay my palms to rest on my thighs.

I notice my keeper nervously wringing his hands beside

me. Maybe I feel a little bad about that. He *is* my keeper and my behavior—good or bad—is ultimately his responsibility in the eyes of the authority. I decide I should play nice for now. My keeper is a little rough around the edges, but he doesn't seem like an altogether awful human being. I'm a little rough around the edges, too, but I'm not completely without conscience. I don't wish harm on the innocent, though knowing who is innocent and who isn't these days can be difficult to discern.

The giant, gorgeous god-man moves around the desk, pulling a drawer open and taking out a single, purple file folder.

"Hey, that matches my hair!" I blurt impulsively, holding out a strand of my violet locks.

His head snaps in my direction to glower at me beneath his thick, dark eyebrows, and I feel a pleasant warmth spread from my belly. His head cocks to the side as he regards me, and I make a show of zipping my fingers across my lips, turning a key at the corner to lock it before tossing it away.

He opens the file and reads aloud as he circles the desk to the front again, casually leaning his ass back on the edge. "Tempest Townsend. Female. Twenty-years-old. Long, purple hair, thick lips, fake lashes."

What the fuck is this?

"Too many ear piercings, black tattoos on her left wrist and forearm. Decent tits, perky round ass. Maybe too edgy for the ordinary winning player, but perhaps just edgy enough for a certain kind of fantasy." He's still reading from the file. "Bad attitude, impulsive, smart mouth. Could probably train that out of her, but otherwise, will play the role of a demon to perfection." He shuts the file and slams it down on the desk behind him. "From your interview, Ms. Townsend. Tell me, if you were an employer and your most trusted employee came to you with interview notes like that, what would you do? Would you have hired that person?"

"Fuck, no." I tell him honestly.

"So, why do you think I approved your hire?"

"Because you recognize an artist when you see one?"

"An artist?" His lips twist into a smile that doesn't touch his eyes. "I don't hire artists; I hire alters."

"Yes, the girls you hired before me were alters, but this one on her knees for you?" I lean forward, pushing my palms down onto my thighs. "She's an artist."

He licks his lips with a thick tongue and my heart thumps an extra beat, my gaze zeroing in on his mouth. "Alters have rules. Rules for serving as angels, and rules for serving as demons."

I tilt my head to the side. "But not really, though."

"Yes, *really*. Do you need another orientation?"

"Would you be the one to orientate me?"

His eyes narrow, scrutinizing me deeply. I can feel his analytical stare cut into my skin, making me bleed vulnerability as he burrows inside me.

Fuck, he's hot.

My fingertips come up to brush across my bottom lip, an obvious tell as instinctive and natural to my lust as wetness dripping from my pussy. His eyes follow the line I draw across my mouth, and he pushes off from the desk.

"Put your fucking hand down."

I slap my hand on my thigh, wet my lips, and do nothing to hide my smirk. He moves toward me, though *moves* doesn't seem like the right word.

He *gravitates* toward me.

Maybe I gravitate toward him and his black hole personality.

I'm a pebble on my knees beneath this redwood tree of a man, whose name I don't even know. "Good girl," he says, and I instantly feel breathless, as if he's just slammed me down on the floor again beneath his boot.

Why do I want him to say that again?

I'm nobody's good girl.

My eyes flicker to his crotch to catch a little peek of the outline of his cock, and *fuck,* maybe I could be a good girl for *that.*

He crosses his arms over his chest and takes a step closer, looking straight down at me and forcing me to crane my neck to look up at him. "Tell me about *Tempest in the Tower.*"

Well, shit.

My face wrinkles, cringing as he outs me. "You found out about that, huh?"

"Did you think we wouldn't?" There's a knock on the door. "Come in," he says, and I whip my head around behind me to look just as the door clicks open.

Three men from the authority in matching black suits walk in. They just need matching sunglasses and they'd be about as intimidating as a little league team—at least their outfits would be on point. One of them comes to stand beside the gorgeous god-man towering over me, while the other two move to grab my keeper and force him to his knees.

"I don't deal well with my employees feeding information to the Syndicate, Tempest."

My neck muscles twitch in horror at the insinuation and my face contorts in contempt. "You're fucking kidding me. I'm not feeding information to the Syndicate. Why would I do that?"

He bends and sinks his fingers into my hair at the crown of my head, jerking my neck back painfully. He holds my stare as he steps closer. His cock is aligned perfectly with my face, and while I should be worried for my *life* right now, I'm lost in a twisted, hopeful desire that he'll take out his dick and choke me with it.

There's something seriously wrong with me.

"You're blasting my secrets all over social media, you stupid, *stupid* girl."

"I'm not blasting secrets. I'm just giving the people what they want."

"How would you know what they want?"

"They just want to know what it's like. They're bored with their pleasant, peaceful, happy little lives out there beyond the city border. They fantasize about an exciting life, though they'd never be fucking strong enough to survive in the city. They just want a glimpse of what it's like for those of us trapped here."

His lips twitch, like a short in his electrical system that I can feel sparking through his tightening grip. But then he tosses me sideways to the floor. I land on my hands as he crosses behind the desk. He pulls open another drawer as I pick myself up and he pulls out a cell phone.

Shit, my cell phone… which I'm not supposed to have.

He starts tapping on the screen and scrolling with his finger. It figures he'd be able to bypass my fingerprint and passcode. "Here's a picture of you in the fucking White Room." He turns the phone to show me the selfie I posted on social media before fucking a winning player maybe a week ago. He turns it back around and starts reading the caption out loud—yikes. "Fucking in the White Room tonight, my favorite. Winning players love me. Hashtag alter life. Hashtag Tower angels. Hashtag the Tower."

"Okay, but, in fairness, that's a really hot picture of me."

He cocks an eyebrow and continues to scroll. "This one you posted from the Red Room, of all places." He shows me and admittedly, I cringe.

"Okay, you've got me on that one. That photo was

probably in poor taste."

It was about two weeks ago, after a particularly brutal session serving as a demon. I didn't think the losing player would spew blood like that when I cut across his neck. I was covered in it from head to toe, crimson spread all over my black leather outfit, dotting my cheeks, and staining my hair. I took the selfie over a pool of blood, holding up the tip of my knife in front of my lips.

"Poor taste?" He laughs, but there is no humor in it. He looks at the screen again and starts to read. "Bloodlust, anyone? It's just my job, but I don't hate it. Safe from the Syndicate here in the Tower, so I guess it's worth taking a life or two. Players know what they're risking when they choose to play. Don't call me the bad guy. Hashtag alter life. Hashtag Tower demons. Hashtag the Tower."

"So… I know it's probably irrelevant. But how did you find out I had a phone in here?"

A dark black flame flashes behind his eyes and he hurtles my phone to the floor between us. I flinch, thinking he's throwing it at me. But when it lands on the floor between us, he lifts his foot and violently stomps down on it, repeatedly, with his heavy black boot. But my eyes are on that hair of his—a thick, dark mop of messy hair, strands bouncing with his brutal movements, just begging for a dumb bitch like me to run her fingers through it.

"How the fuck did you get that phone in here? How did you even get it in the first place?"

"You may not know this, mister high and mighty, but everyone on the street has a phone. The Syndicate likes the drama of social media."

He rushes for me, bending low, putting his face in front of mine, and forcing me to lean back. "I *know* they like the drama. We stay out of their drama. It's the only reason they let me run my business how I see fit. It's the *only* fucking reason my girls are protected."

I put my hand on my heart and gasp. "Are you calling me your girl?"

A tight smile tugs at the corners of his lips as his eyes flicker down in frustration before lifting again, meeting me with an intense stare. "One of many, baby doll. But now I'm forced to reconsider your employment. You've unwittingly given the Syndicate a glimpse into Heaven and the Hellscape."

"I'm confused," I tell him honestly. "I thought the Syndicate knew everything about the Tower."

"They know what I *tell* them, Tempest. And now they know what you've *shown* them."

"*If* they saw my account."

"One point eight million followers, you fucking dumb slut."

"Ooh, bend me over and spank me next time you call me that, *daddy*." I lift my hand between our faces and give him my middle finger to highlight the displeasure on my face at his choice of words. We're so close that my knuckle grazes the tip of his nose.

He snatches my wrist and I'm certain he's going to break my arm. I brace myself for the pain, knowing I probably deserve it for being such a brat, but it doesn't come. Instead, he sucks my middle finger between his lips.

My body slumps.

I'm weightless.

All my essence and energy rushes straight to my pussy, and my whole body sinks toward it. He's practically holding me up by the wrist, and I don't even fucking care.

Who the fuck is this guy?

Then, the pain comes.

He bites down on my finger, *hard*, actually causing me to yelp. When he slowly drags my hand away from his mouth, he lets his sunk-in teeth graze my finger, digging and scraping with force over my skin. I can feel my face contort from the pain that's both bruising and stinging at the same time.

"You need to learn your place." He licks his lips and stands, turning away from me, and I finally feel like I can take a deep breath. "You compromised our integrity. There's a reason we do a strip search when you arrive to work here. There's a reason alters stay in the Tower instead of being allowed to return to whatever piece of shit home they have out there. It's not because I'm generous, though you'll find that I am more than I should be. It's for everyone's protection—mine, yours, the players, the keepers." He turns toward my keeper and takes a few steps closer to him. "Keepers are responsible for their alters, day and night. If an alter is out of line, it's the fault of the keeper. He must bear that responsibility."

"If you had any idea what I deal with…" my keeper says. "She's a fucking challenge."

"Are you not capable of handling a tiny girl with purple hair?"

Ooh, he likes my hair.

"I'm capable, it's just—"

"No excuses. Do you even know who I am?"

"You're… you're one of the authority," the keeper stammers.

He shakes his head, perfect hair waving in clean, bouncy strands. "No. *They* are the authority." He indicates the men in the black suits.

I narrow my eyes in consideration of this at the same time my keeper does. The god-man isn't wearing the same black suit the authority always wears. He's not wearing the obligatory gray button-up and black slacks like the keepers. He's in a simple black T-shirt, faded and ripped skinny jeans, and black combat boots. He's dressed like someone else entirely.

If he's not the authority, then he must be…

"I'm the fucking Deity."

I sink back on my heels, my breath escaping me in a rush. "Holy shit."

He's the Deity… the motherfucking Deity.

Never in my life did I dream I would get to see him.

He's had his hands on me.

He touched me!

I hold up my hand in front of my face and look at the bite marks he left on my middle finger.

He marked me.

I'm marked by the Deity, and I could practically burst with excitement. My keeper, on the other hand, doesn't look quite so happy.

The Deity—*oh, my God, the Deity*—bends, pulls his knife from the calf holster strapped around his tight jeans, and goes after my poor, innocent keeper. I watch with unblinking eyes as my keeper fights the two authority, who hold him down by his shoulders. He shouts, begging for mercy, actually telling the Deity to kill *me* instead for my indiscretion.

Rude.

But the Deity doesn't even hesitate. He draws his arm across his chest and, with a quick, even slice, cuts across my keeper's throat. Blood sprays from him, bursting from the cut and splashing all over the Deity. He doesn't flinch away from it, doesn't move back to avoid it. He stands there— tall, proud, strong—letting the blood soak him entirely. I feel drops of it splash across my face and chest, but I'm far enough away that it doesn't drench me.

Blood pours from the keeper as the men holding him

finally let go. He tilts sideways and lands on the floor with a thud. I watch his neck as his crimson life force continues to pulse from his gaping wound, spurt after spurt blasting out more of it with each slowing beat of his dying heart.

I feel weird about it, wrong about it, but since I started working as an alter, I've become just a little bit fascinated by blood. It's not that I was ever a particularly morbid person. I do actually feel bad about my keeper because it wasn't his fault I was snapping selfies and posting them without his knowledge. It's not like I want to go off killing people just to get off on it like a fucking psycho serial killer or something. It's just that the concept of it is so intriguing…

It's the idea that we all have this liquid trapped inside our fragile bodies, liquid that's responsible for keeping us alive, rushing beneath our breakable skin that can be sliced so easily to free it from within us. Our hearts keep working to pump it through our veins, even when a vein has been severed, instead pumping the blood faster outside of us and forcing us to our deaths quicker.

Blood and life and death—these are things I've become more and more curious about the more I serve as a demon.

I'm staring so intently at the blood flowing from my keeper, that somehow, I didn't notice the Deity move in close to me again. My eyes turn from the keeper on the floor and land first on the Deity's black combat boots, almost completely covered, smeared red streaks that drip to the floor.

I have an odd sudden urge that I could try to force from my mind, but I don't. I think perhaps I've lost my mind, but fuck, I'm going with it, because I'm nothing if not impulsive and reckless.

Go big or go home, right?

I bend forward, place my palms on the floor, and run my tongue over the top of his boot, picking up the metallic taste of blood as I draw a path up to his laces—and if I'm just being honest here, blood tastes fucking disgusting, and I clearly didn't think this one through.

I stop at his laces, realizing the room has gone unnaturally quiet and still. I raise my head to look up at him as I sit back on my heels. I use my teeth to scrape the overwhelming amount of blood forward, to the tip of my tongue, and then spit it on the floor beside me.

"Well, that was a little tangier than I expected." I shrug, blinking up at him with innocent eyes.

What's even more unexpected than me licking the blood off his boot is his reaction to it. He crouches to his haunches in front of me, dangling his dripping knife from his fingers in the space between us. Blood streaks across his cheeks and soaks his shirt.

"I should kill you, Tempest."

I swallow hard, some of the blood thickly creeping down the back of my throat and it's quite disgusting.

I don't want to die.

I don't want to lose this job.

I don't want to go back to where I came from.

Obviously, I should have thought about all that before sneaking in a cell phone and posting pictures from inside the Tower on social media that the whole damn world can see. I'm great at understanding my failings and bad decisions after the fact, but terrible at doing it in the moment.

I straighten my spine, lift my chin, and stare intently into his eyes. "You could kill me, and maybe you should. But I don't think you really want to do that. Your winning players know about me. I'm different, unique. They want that. They want *me.* I've been an angel more frequently than a demon because they *request* me. Even the losing players can appreciate their death being handed to them by a girl like me, don't you think?" I lift my eyebrow, angling my head to the side just a smidgen. "I'm irreplaceable."

A hint of a smirk tugs up at the corner of his mouth. "The only irreplaceable person in this Tower is *me,* Tempest."

I lean forward. "I can help stroke that ego of yours if it gets too hard, lover."

I see a flash of light behind his dark eyes, but perhaps I'm only imagining it. He pushes to his feet and turns away. I tense up, thinking he's about to whip his arm around and slice my throat, just like he did to my keeper.

"Take him out of here," he says to the authority, and they move to drag the body from the room. "I think you're fucking nuts."

"Thank you," I say quickly, wishing I knew how to keep

my mouth shut.

He whirls around to look at me. "I'm putting you on probation."

"Probation?"

"No more phone, no more social media."

"No more keeper?"

He shakes his head. "No more keeper."

My eyes widen in surprise. I was just joking.

How the hell can I be kept as an alter without a keeper?

He strides back to stand in front of me, reaching down to place two fingers beneath my chin, lifting my head. "I wouldn't dare give you an inch after the shit you've pulled." He puts his hand on the top of my head and strokes down my hair, surely streaking it with the blood covering his fingers. "You don't need another keeper because now, you have my attention. You're mine now, baby doll, and I'm not taking my eyes off you."

CHAPTER THREE
shower buddy

"GET UP," HE orders.

I climb to my feet, my legs moving to his command before my mind can catch up and decide otherwise.

I don't even have a smart-ass response for a simple order from him. The Deity is different, special… and not just because of who he is. There's something about him I can't quite place, but it's something that almost makes me want to fight my impulsive instincts and try to behave.

I want to impress him, of course—he's the Deity, for crying out loud.

I wait for him to command me again, finding that I'm also looking forward to it, and that's so fucking unusual for me because I don't tend to do well with authority these days.

He pauses, standing in front of me, watching me. His

eyes draw a line from the top of my head to my toes and all the way back up again. His head is inclined to the side as he regards me with his distant, dark, brooding eyes. The longer he looks, the stronger I feel his pull, the gravity of him tugging me, pulling me, stretching me toward his dark oblivion.

It feels fucking good.

"You have a new assignment tonight."

"Oh?"

His tongue sneaks out to wet his lips, a swift and intentional flick like a snake showing me his agitation, as if he feels threatened by my presence, as if I'm a danger to him and he's preparing to coil around me, sink his teeth into me, inject me with his deadly venom.

I don't think his venom would kill me.

There's already poison in my veins from the brutal chaos of the life forced upon us by the Syndicate.

"Come with me," he says, then turns.

He strides across his office, forming a dark silhouette to the vision of the city outside the picture window. As he moves, I watch him, unashamedly checking out his beautiful ass in his perfectly fitting jeans.

I'm having a hard time guessing his age—I always pictured the haughty, pretentious Deity of the Tower to be a middle-aged man in a tailored suit with a penchant for power. But the man in front of me couldn't possibly be more than a decade older than my twenty years, if that, and he seems more concerned with maintaining control amidst the chaos than he does in being the powerful, spotlighted figurehead of the city's infamous Tower.

He heads straight toward a built-in bookcase along the far wall and stops in front of it. He grabs hold of the side of the shelf and tugs. It swings open on a slow hinge, the bookshelf plastered to the wall in such a way that one would never know it's a hidden door without being shown.

He walks through, and from where I'm standing, I can see there's an entire living space beyond it. He takes a few steps into the hidden penthouse, but stops when he realizes I haven't followed. He turns, comes back to the threshold, and demands every ounce of his attention with a single look. I start walking without another word from him, and I find a whole new world beyond the bookshelf door.

A penthouse apartment suite.

Pristinely clean, neat, and white.

My feet pad across white marbled floors that cover the entire flat expanse in front of me. There's a large white dining table to my left beneath a crystalline chandelier. Straight ahead is a kitchen, with white counters, white cabinets, chrome fixtures and door pulls, and a massive island defining the space.

Another large picture window lines the expanse from behind the dining table and beyond, lining the apartment from one end to the other. There's almost nothing I wouldn't give to live in a space with a window like this—the view is mind-blowing.

I see a living room past the kitchen, which is furnished with a white couch, white chairs, white rug…

Everything is *white*.

Even the artwork hung on the walls is a boring mixture of neutrals—blacks and grays splashed and streaked on a white canvas.

He must have a thing for angels.

I suppose it makes sense that the Deity would live in a space that looks like heaven. But it's such a jarring contrast to see the pristine white smeared with the blood dripping from him as he strides toward the exposed, chrome metal staircase on our right.

Who knew you could bleed in heaven?

I suppose even God himself isn't immune to the atrocities of humanity.

He trudges up the steps, seemingly unconcerned about the mess he's making. I follow him, my heart pumping eagerly. I'm a little bit afraid of him, if for no other reason than the fact that I've angered him with my social media posts, knowing he could take me out with a single swipe of the blade he still holds.

I step from the staircase onto the second floor and my feet land on more white marble flooring. It's cold here—I never would have imagined it would be cold in such a heavenly-looking space.

Shouldn't heaven be warm and welcoming?

This space is anything but that.

Cold.

Hard.

Overwhelming.

The white overwhelms me. My eyes search for color and find the blood trail of his boot imprints. The blood gives me comfort, as fucked-up as that is. It warms the space, making my sinner's heart feel worthy of being here.

I follow the Deity to a white master bedroom, and we pass through it quickly into an attached master bathroom.

White, white, fucking white.

I stop, standing still beside the sink as he turns to face me. His eyes find mine and hold me darkly, my fear finally giving way in the comfort of his darkness, in the contrast he brings to this heavenly space.

"I want to see you in action," he says as he tugs his shirt up over his head and tosses it onto the floor.

I'm speechless.

Actually, fucking speechless.

I *always* have something to say.

Why aren't there any words coming out of my smart mouth?

"I'm re-assigning you to the Red Room tonight." He kicks off his boots. "Consider it a chance to prove yourself worthy of serving me." He unbuckles his belt, his jeans, and before I even realize what he's doing, he's stark naked in front of me. Bare flesh, bronzed skin, rippling hard body— the body of a god—and blood.

Flesh and blood.

And a monster fucking cock.

My knees buckle, my clenching core urging me to get on my knees and worship him. Instead, I reach over and put my hand on the counter to steady myself. His face is hard and unreadable. I fucking hate that, but shit, the mystery makes me wet.

"Did you clean yourself up after the White Room?"

"Unfortunately, no." I jut out my hip with my fist resting against it. "I didn't have time since the authority pulled me out as soon as the old guy came inside me."

His nostrils flare and he tilts his head back toward the shower behind him. "Get in."

"Well, aren't we getting familiar?" I push off the counter and move right on past him. "Would you like to do the honor of undressing me, or should I do that myself?" I wait, but he just stares back at me blankly, a quizzical look on his face. He's not the first person to give me that *what-the-fuck-is-wrong-with-you* expression.

I pull open the glass shower door and step inside, eager to take off the thigh-highs that keep bunching around my knees. The disgustingly soaked panties come off next, followed by the bralette, and then, I'm unashamedly naked in his shower.

"Sixty seconds. Hurry the fuck up," he says from the other side of the glass enclosure.

I'm accustomed to quick showers on angel nights—a

clean cunt between each winner is a requirement. Sometimes I see as many as four players in a row. And because I'll be glad to wash the remnants of the last one away, I happily turn on the flow and get to cleaning. I watch him as I soap up, but it's highly disappointing because he won't look away from my face.

Hello? Are you a man? Look at my killer rack!

The moment I'm finished with the most basic cleanse ever, he rips open the door. "Time's up. Get out."

"Fuck, I hope you don't finish that quickly in bed." I step out of the shower, and he shoves a blindingly white towel into my hands. He finally gives me a quick once-over, and I detect the tiniest hint of interest.

"You'll stand right there while I shower so I can keep my eyes on you. You won't move and you won't do anything stupid. Do you understand?"

"Are you sure you don't need a shower buddy? I make a great shower buddy."

There—a flicker, a hint of amusement twitching at the corner of his mouth.

"I don't need anything other than your silence."

"You can always gag me."

Nothing.

No reaction.

He just turns, pulls open the clear glass shower door, steps inside, and shuts it behind him. The water pours from the waterfall spout overhead. Two side spouts built into the white tile shower walls blast water directly at his chiseled abs.

Why is my pulse racing?

Why is my heart pounding?

Why does my soul scream to be near him, to touch him, to please him?

I step forward, closing the distance to the glass enclosure. I watch the blood thin and fade to a dark pink as the water dilutes it, pushing it in streams down his body to the shower floor. I watch as it circles the drain and disappears. I watch as he cleanses himself, washing himself clean of the mess I made.

Because I'm the one who made this mess for him.

That blood is on my hands.

I want him to cleanse my hands of this, too—to scrub them clean over the ripples of his muscles, to let the waterfall rinse the blood from him, and then we can both be rid of the burden.

He turns and faces me, as if he senses how close I'm standing now, as if he expected it. Only the glass door separates me from the Deity. His eyes take hold of mine and they don't let go. My fingers find their way to my bottom lip and brush across it.

I'm panting, breathless as I watch him watch me.

I don't understand why he's looking at me at all. I'm just another one of his alters, and an alter who has been causing him trouble, at that. His chest rises and falls in heavy breaths, and my inhales and exhales race to sync with his.

I move my hand from my mouth and rest my fingertips on the glass door. I don't know why I'm reaching out to him; I just know that I can't look away, can't walk away, can't stop the tingling in my core.

He takes a slow, calculated step backward. His eyes leave mine for a second, only long enough to glance down at his cock in an intentional move to draw my attention there, too.

It works, obviously.

I couldn't possibly miss the way his cock thickens and grows hard.

Fuck, is that for me?

Does he want me?

He leans back against the tiled wall and grasps his cock with a firm hand, stroking forward to the tip. My knees go a little weak again, and suddenly, I feel like a needy puppy pawing at the door, urgently trying to get to its master for pets and cuddles and fucking belly rubs.

I want his hands on me.

The towel drops from my hands to the floor and both my palms press to the glass as he strokes, as he works himself into a state of pure need. I'm hoping, praying he'll lose control, grab me, pull me in, bend me over, and fuck me.

When he's worked us both into a frenzy of panting, heart-pounding, hard, wet lust, he steps forward, resting his forehead against the glass.

Our eyes lock. "You want it, don't you?"

I nod, unable to speak over the heat, woozy from the steam that swirls around the space.

"You haven't earned it, baby doll. And I doubt you ever will."

He turns, faces away from me, toward the shower wall. He braces a hand against it, hiding his cock from me as he strokes. I see his muscles flex and tense as he forces himself closer and closer to the edge of release. He doesn't let me see his face when he spills his cum over the tiles.

The denial reminds me of my place, reminds me that I'm less than, small in his eyes, unworthy of witnessing something so precious as the Deity's pleasure.

And it makes me want him that much more.

CHAPTER FOUR
brutal inhumanity

THE RED ROOM is in the basement of the Tower because that's just fitting as fuck. The Deity and I stopped briefly on the twentieth floor, where the alters stay, so I could change into an outfit more befitting a demon. Black corset, cinched to discomfort, black leather miniskirt, and combat boots over my snagged and tattered fishnets.

My make-up required a quick update from my angel look, too. I darkened the shadow and liner around my eyes, popped in my silver contact lenses for that extra bit of creepy, and painted my lips a dark burgundy.

The Deity and I ride the elevator in tense silence. It's tense for me, at least, maybe not so much for him. He seems perfectly calm and cool while I stand beside him, a horny, needy bundle of nerves that wants to pull up her skirt and bend over for him.

I know he won't fuck me like that, though. He'd see me as a weak little girl who just wants attention. A part of me *is* a weak little girl who just wants attention, but that's not the sum of my existence.

I'm more than that.

I want him to know I'm more than that.

I want him to keep me around, for my safety, of course… but maybe for more.

The elevator doors open to the black hallway of the Hellscape, and the familiar red neon lights flicker as we step off the elevator. I can already hear the screaming—must be a busy night on the Tower gambling floor. I hear no less than three shouting, begging, losing players behind the multiple doors that line the hall.

This is where alters serve as demons. Most of the rooms here are similar, with a table in the center that's affixed with leather straps to hold down the losers. Each room has various tools and implements for the alters to use as they torture and torment and ultimately kill. But the Red Room is the biggest with the most versatility. It's where they take the players who gambled big and lost even bigger. That's where we're going tonight.

I follow the Deity to the end of the hall, and he pushes the door open for me, standing in the threshold with his hand on the doorknob as I pass through. He smells like hellfire, a flame I'd like to burn me.

The Red Room is a large rectangular space with red walls and black marble flooring. There's a table in every room in the Hellscape, but the one in the Red Room is special. The other rooms have fixed, stationary tables, but this one tilts in all directions—it even has the capability to invert the player so his head points toward the floor. It allows alters some creativity in their demon play.

It's a room fit for an artist.

Like me.

The Deity walks to the far corner of the room, turns his back to it, crosses his arms, and silently waits. It's exactly what every keeper does for his alter. They're here for protection, for an extra set of hands to help with the heavy lifting, to support us in carrying out our duties and to make sure we leave our nightly work unharmed. It's how I have to think of him tonight as I work—as a keeper, rather than the Deity himself.

I feel a little nauseous at the thought of him watching me work. He's the Deity, for crying out loud. Never in a million years could I have predicted meeting him.

No one has met him.

No one knows who he is.

Anyone walking into this room would just think he's a new keeper, and I have no desire to divulge that secret to anyone. This secret makes me feel special and I'm going to keep it.

"I won't tell anyone who you are," I offer as I lean

against the counter's edge, looking at him from across the empty table in the center of the gloomy space.

"I'm not concerned. No one would believe you if you told them, anyway."

"You're probably right."

I'm not exactly a fan favorite among the other alters. I'm friendly enough with a few of them, but some of them think I'm a creepy attention whore—which, to be fair, I am—but this is one thing I don't want to use for attention.

Shocking, I know.

I want the Deity all to myself and that feels so at odds with my natural impulses. I should want to shout it from the rooftop that I have the Deity's attention, that he's watching me, that in some small way, he's threatened enough by my presence to act as my temporary keeper. But the way he looks at me feels personal and I'm afraid I'll lose that look if I tell.

Why am I afraid of that?

"Have you ever done this before?" I ask.

"What?"

"Been in the Red Room? Watched an alter work as a demon?"

"I see everything that happens in the Tower."

I scrunch my face, tilting my head a little in disbelief. "*Everything?* You can't possibly see everything."

"I'm the fucking Deity."

"Right, sure, but you're not some floating mystical

being that can be in all places at once."

His eyebrows furrow, hooding his eyes. "I see every little thing you do, Tempest." The way he says it is so clear, so precise, so insistent, that I have no choice but to believe it.

Our conversation ends when I hear our losing player shout from the hallway. It's a familiar song and dance. It's the distant sound of the elevator doors sliding shut behind him as he's pulled off, followed by the *ding* as it's sent back up for the next. It's the sound of fists and nails colliding and grasping at drywall, shoes scuffing against the marble floor, screams and shouts in protest as he's dragged toward our room by the authority.

I push off the counter and walk around to the other side of the table, facing the doorway, so I can watch as they bring him in.

This part isn't exactly my favorite.

Violence is just a part of life in the city and that violence doesn't end at the Tower doors. The difference between the streets and the Tower is sequence, routine, security, expectation. Though most of the men who willingly enter the Tower to gamble are innocent civilians, they know damn well what they're risking when they come in here—they know the consequences if they lose their bets.

I may be twisted, but I'm not blind to the brutal inhumanity of it all. When you live in a locked-down city ruled by cruel, vicious men, you have to create your own definition of humane. It's kill or be killed out there, and it's no different in the Tower.

This isn't the kind of job you get fired from for doing poorly—it's a *sign-on-for-life* kind of job. The benefit of living is the greatest compensation the Tower offers, and I'd be a fool to give that up.

Most people would be surprised to learn how quickly one can normalize brutality when their life depends on it. I've adapted, accepted, come to terms with the demon game I have to play to stay.

The authority drags in a fighting man, bringing him over to the table. The Deity—my keeper for the evening—approaches to assist the authority in lifting the thirty-something, brown-haired man onto the table and strapping him down. Once he's secure, the Deity steps back and the two men of the authority give him a knowing nod of respect. They don't normally recognize the keeper at all, so this tells me that at least the authority knows the identity of the Deity.

I look down at the average-looking man on the table and take in a deep, steadying breath. I can feel the Deity's eyes on me, boring a hole through the back of my skull. It gives me goosebumps and makes my skin tingle in a sinful sort of way. It's a little off-putting that his stare alone sparks excitement—it's excitement that shouldn't be present before I'm about to torture the fuck out of this guy.

With a forced exhale, I shed the anxiety of my

conscience for what I'm about to do. I temporarily rid myself of emotion and slip into the demon role I have to play for my own survival.

"So..." I start, blinking my silver demon eyes at the strapped-down player. "Are you a drag it out, build anticipation kind of guy, or should we just jump right into the deep end?"

I lean away just in time to avoid the spit he forcefully ejects in the direction of my face.

Gross.

"Deep end it is," I decide.

I circle the table, moving back around to the counter along the side wall and pull open a drawer. This drawer is filled with sharp instruments, things to cut and slice with. If I have to torture someone, this is the best way to do it, in my opinion. Some of the alters spend their time breaking fingers and toes, using electrocution, whipping, flogging, waterboarding, but I find those things uninspiring.

It's blood that gives us life, and draining it slowly takes that life away. I can't think of a more effective way to fuck with someone than to make them watch their own blood drip out onto the floor. I can't think of a torture worse than watching your own life slowly seep away.

It's fucked up.

It's been a little horrifying to live the transition of my mind as it learns to accept this violence, but even worse to become slowly more fascinated by it.

It's the job.

That's what I always have to remind myself.

I choose a nine-inch hunting knife because this one is the most intimidating for the losing players to see. They know that one stab to their midsection with such a long, wide blade could instantly cause irreparable damage, making the reality of their death all the more real.

When I turn around, knife in hand, I jump in surprise to see the Deity standing there on the opposite side of the table, looking down at the losing player as though the sight of him was the most interesting thing in the world.

I take a step forward and he lifts his head, catching my eyes with a flicker of flame that sparks between us—it heats the air and catches fire. He doesn't move away from the table as I approach. I'm curious to know what he's expecting from me… if he wants me to do something different tonight.

He nods toward the player. "Go on."

Air catches in my lungs at the deepness of his tone. I step forward. Only the player separates me from the Deity. I grab the hem of the player's T-shirt, slip the knife beneath it, and split the fabric down the middle to expose his chest and abdomen.

That's when he loses it.

This is the moment he realizes this is really happening to him. He thrashes against the leather straps that bind him to the table. He screams, he shouts, he crumbles into a begging, sobbing mess of a man who desperately wants to cling to life.

I lean over him, putting my face close to his, making sure he sees my eyes. "It's nothing personal, you know. You don't have to hate me for doing this to you. Honestly," I shrug, tilting my head, "you should probably hate *yourself* for this. Gambling at the Tower is pretty fucking stupid, right? Unless you win, of course. But you didn't. So, instead of getting to fuck me in Heaven, you're down here in the Hellscape, getting tortured. Kind of a mind fuck, am I right? But good on you for trying." I pat his chest condescendingly.

"I just needed more rations!" he shouts.

I straighten. "Yeah, don't you all? Gambling tip for next time? Don't lose. Oh, shit… I guess there won't be a next time for you." I lift my hands with a shrug. "Sorry."

"Stop playing and cut him," the Deity commands.

My head jerks to look at him, surprised by this. "We're supposed to play—"

"I know what you're supposed to do; I wrote the playbook. But I want to see you cut him. *Now.*"

I hold my breath while he speaks, unintentionally, of course. He's insistent with his words, with his posture, with his eyes. I swallow, my mouth suddenly dry. His perfect pout speaks to me without any words at all, as if he's inside my head, telling me what he wants me to do, commanding me like only a god could. I lift my knife, gently press the tip to the center of the man's chest, push down lightly, and drag it down to his belly button.

He screams, his entire body tense and rigid against the pain. Blood seeps from the line I draw with my blade, dripping down both sides of his torso. I lift my knife and stand still, watching the blood flow out of him, fascinated by the way it leaves his body… like it was only waiting to be freed.

Why does our blood flow so easily?

It almost puts me in a trance between the screaming and the slowly flowing crimson. I'm startled from my thoughts by the voice of the Deity, but he's no longer across the table. He's standing right behind me.

"Do you enjoy this?" he asks.

I take in a shaky breath. "Do I enjoy what?"

"The blood. Do you enjoy watching it spill?" I can feel the force of him as he takes a step closer.

"Enjoy isn't the right word."

"What is?"

"It makes me feel… curious."

"Curious," he repeats.

His hands clutch my biceps. The touch should make me tense up; it should make me nervous. But instead, it relaxes me, and I melt in the grip of his large, strong hands.

"How…" I hesitate. "How does it make *you* feel?"

His body molds against my back, standing impossibly close. "Violence is power in the Syndicate's world."

"It makes you feel powerful to watch an innocent man bleed and die?"

"No. It makes me feel powerful to watch a woman like you—a woman whose days were numbered on the streets—flourish in the power I've granted her. I've given you this power. I've given you the ability to assert your will over weak-minded men who gambled their luck and fucking lost. Men who might have taken advantage of a pretty thing like you had they met you alone on the street. Cut him again, Tempest."

Oh, fuck.

The way he says my name has my pussy clenching. He oozes power, and I'm fucking high on it. His hands trail down my arms, gripping just past my elbows. His grip remains firm as I raise my hand, put the tip of the knife at the man's belly button, and run a quick diagonal slice toward his side.

His piercing scream makes me jump—I'm fucking jittery in the Deity's hold. I'm not a jittery person, but his touch, his presence… it puts me on edge. It's an edge I want him to push me off from so I can free fall through this power-high.

He's right. Whether I'm serving as an angel or a demon, it does make me feel more powerful. It gives me a scrap of control in a world where I feel otherwise vulnerable.

"Who *are* you?" he asks, and he sounds genuinely curious, as if he doesn't know. He presses in closer, his body pushing me forward until my stomach bumps into the side of the table.

"I'm…" I hesitate unnaturally, unsure of how to answer, but somehow knowing exactly what I need to say—the truth. "I'm your angel. Your demon. Your fucking disciple."

His hands leave me, but in a single motion, he fists my hair at the base of my skull and forces my head down, bending me over the losing player on the table. I turn my face just in time for my cheek to land against the man's stomach, against his gaping, bleeding wounds. I squeeze my eyes shut against the thick blood smearing my cheek as the Deity bends over me. The pressure of him—his cock against my ass, his threatening hand in my hair—makes me shamelessly wet.

Deliberately, I spread my legs wider.

"You belong to me. I own you." His other hand sneaks between us, reaching down to cup my pussy beneath my leather miniskirt, digging in with the heel of his palm and making me gasp. "Is this wet mess all for me, baby doll?"

"Yes," I whimper.

"Do you want me to fuck you?"

"Yes."

"Do you want me to make you come?"

"*Fuck*, yes."

"Have you earned it?"

"I mean, probably not, but can I just have it, anyway? I'll make it up to you."

I'm yanked upright in a flash as he tugs back on my hair, spinning me around to face him. He stays close, pinning my ass against the edge of the table with his hard body. I blink rapidly as blood drips down my forehead, slipping over my eyelid, threatening to cloud my vision. He reaches up and places his palm on the side of my face, brushing his thumb across my eye and wiping the blood away. My heart starts pounding, the rush of his gentle touch on my cheek contrasting with his formidable presence.

"This means nothing," he says.

I open my mouth to ask him what he means, but he devours my words with his warm lips on mine. Heat and power fill my lungs as he feeds me the air I need to breathe.

Holy fucking hell.

Who is this man?

I think he might be an actual fucking god.

I'm only vaguely aware that the man on the table behind me is sobbing and whimpering as the Deity kisses me roughly. My focus is intent, my body fully aware in the arms of this god-like man who makes my soul throb. My lips tingle, my tongue aches from battling his, my heart hammers, my nipples harden, my stomach clenches, and wetness soaks me between my legs.

I have never—*never*—been this tuned-in and turned-on in my life.

Never.

He breaks the kiss with a jarring abruptness that holds me in limbo, somewhere between reality and fantasy. He pants, staring down at me, chest lifting and lowering in rapid, shallow breaths. He looks nearly manic, unhinged but controlled, needy but commanding.

He straightens, pulling away from me. "You taste like sin."

My knees weaken and I slump against the table. "What does that mean?"

"It means you're a dangerous woman, *Tempest in the Tower*." He takes a step back and my eyes dip to see that he does, in fact, have a hard-on from that kiss—I fucking *knew* it. "Dangerous women need to be shown their place in my tower."

I spin, put my hands on the table beside the bleeding man and arch my back, pushing my ass out toward the Deity, and glancing at him over my shoulder. "Please, *please* put me in my place."

I'm not sure exactly how I expected him to react, but I sure as fuck didn't expect him to take the bait. He steps in close, draws his palm up the back of my thigh, running over my torn fishnets. His fingers creep up the hem of my skirt. His touch leaves me, but returns instantly with a hard smack, flat against my cheek. I yelp, rocking forward, my skin stinging from his touch. Heat radiates outward from the point of contact, burning and tingling and drawing my attention to that single painful spot.

Fuck… Do it again.

I feel his fingertips brush across my ass and instinctively tense against the touch with the anticipation of more pleasurable pain, but it doesn't come. He yanks my skirt back down in place and moves around the table, back to the far corner of the room.

I watch as he brings his arms across his chest, leans back against the wall with one of his boots pressed to it beside his knee. His sizable erection must be painful against those tight jeans, and I can't stop myself from thinking about freeing it.

"Tempest," he commands, and my eyes are drawn back up to his face. "Finish your job."

With a heavy sigh, I turn my knife on the man on my table, position it over his abdomen to avoid any damage that will kill him instantly, and force it down deep inside him. I watch the blood ooze, force myself to focus on the screaming, the acknowledgment that I'm doing my job well, and pretend that I'm not feeling things I'm not allowed to feel toward the Deity.

There's more to the tingling, heart-pounding, aching need to please than just lust. I feel the pull deep inside my soul, and in his eyes, I see that he feels it, too.

I know he's right.

That makes me a dangerous fucking woman.

And I have no doubt he'll put me in my place.

CHAPTER FIVE
be a good girl

IN THE CORNER of the Deity's bedroom is a large wooden chair resembling a throne fit for an inmate's execution. He gestures to the chair, which is angled toward his bed. "Have a seat."

After I finished with the losing player in the Red Room, he brought me back here to his penthouse suite on the thirtieth floor. He let me use the bathroom, but gave me no time to shower and clean-up after the bloody mess I made—highly unusual, as thorough cleansing after demon play was always required by my keeper before.

I move toward the hard chair, surprised I hadn't noticed it earlier. It's a massive seat, probably twice as wide as my ass, and all harsh angles. It looks horribly uncomfortable, with no cushioning, no comfort. It's just hard, black wood sitting ominously in the corner.

I brush my fingertips along the straight, flat line of the armrest. "I'd probably be more comfortable on the bed."

"Sit in the fucking chair."

My shoulders jump at the forcefulness of his tone. "All right. Don't get your panties in a wad." I turn around in front of the seat and gradually lower, anxiety over his intentions creeping through my limbs.

"Scoot your ass against the back. Sit up straight." He steps closer, moving to loom above me at the side of the throne.

I do as I'm told, flattening my spine to the hard back. The rigid wood is uncomfortable to sit upright against, and I hope I'm not going to be here for long.

Wishful thinking, right?

"Arms up."

I look up at him sideways as he pulls a leather strap attached by a chain to the top corner of the chair. "Ooh, kinky," I quip, and give him my arm.

He wraps the leather cuff around my wrist, pulling it tight and latching the buckle. He lets go and my arm dangles from the high chair back, my elbow forming a right angle from my shoulder as the chain doesn't leave enough give for me to drop my arm any further. He moves to the other side of the chair, and we repeat the same song and dance—I give him my arm and he locks in my wrist.

He doesn't look at me as he latches me to the chair. It

makes me feel uneasy, but also excited. I'm itching to know what this is all about—what he uses this chair for, why he's putting me in it, what he really wants from me.

I give a tug on both arms, testing the restraints. The leather sticks firmly to my skin, my wrists positively locked in and the chains giving little leeway for movement as they clank against the wood. Fuck, my shoulders will be tired before long in this position.

"Legs up."

"Excuse me?"

"Legs. Up. On the armrests."

"You want me to spread my legs for you, over the armrests?"

"Do you understand words, or do I need to draw you a fucking picture?"

"Yes, *thank* you. Please draw me a kinky picture of how you want my legs spread for you on the armrests."

There's a tick in his cheeks, like his lips want to curl into a smile, but he fights it. Warmth spreads through my chest. That little tick, the hint of a possibility that I might amuse him, entertain him, *interest* him… it makes me fucking hot.

He doesn't ask me again. He grabs my left leg just behind the knee, raises it from the seat, and hitches it up and over the solid wooden armrest. A heavy rush of breath escapes my lungs when his fingers dig into my flesh with that aching, bruising, careless sort of touch that I'm learning he does so well.

The harsh edge of the armrest digs into my flesh, and I'm antsy to put my leg down. But then he brings out a leather strap from beneath the chair. It's not attached to anything—it's really just a shortened belt. He loops it beneath the open square that the armrest forms with the seat and positions my leg so my calf rests straight on top of the armrest. He hooks the buckle of the strap over my shin, and with a sharp yank, tightens it painfully.

"Fuck!" I shout as the wood squeezes against my calf muscle.

He moves to the other side and grabs my right leg, hoisting it up and over the same way, locking me in place. My breaths are heavy as my brain processes that this is both super sexy and super dangerous. The Deity has me completely at his mercy and I know nothing about him.

Don't I, though?

I kind of feel like I know him.

There's fear creeping around in my mind, and it puts me on edge. I feel hot, wet, horny, and terrified all at once. But I refuse to let my fear show, so I do what I normally do when I'm feeling defensive and descend into sarcasm and goading.

I put on a little girl voice. "What are you gonna do to me, daddy?"

"Don't call me that." He crouches to his haunches right in front of me, regarding me like a delicious piece of meat he's just thrown on the grill.

"Then what do I call you? The Deity? I don't even know your name." I lean my head forward sharply, though my arms stay rooted behind me. "Tell me your name."

"Why do you want to know my name?"

"I don't know." I lean back, letting my head touch the back of the chair and smirk. "So I can use it against you?"

He shoots forward, his hand reaching out with a snap to wrap around the back of my neck, dragging me forward again. He pulls hard, my shoulders and biceps stretching behind me, my shoulder blades pinching sharply at the center of my back. A puff of breath escapes my parted lips as he places his forehead against mine, piercing me with his dark, dangerous stare.

"You know what, baby doll? I'm gonna tell you my name."

"You are?"

"Yes. Because no one in the Tower knows my name. Not a single soul inside this building."

I'm breathless in his grip, panting against the stretching, pulling ache in my arms and upper back. "Then why tell me?"

"If I tell you my name, and I hear it uttered from any other lips but yours, then I'll know you were the one who told my secret. If anyone else speaks my name, I'll know your betrayal and you won't survive more than an hour after that. Do you understand me? I'll take you to the Syndicate myself, offer you up as a ritual sacrifice, and let them slaughter you, little lamb."

"Never mind. I don't really need to know your name," I reply with wide eyes—I'm not exactly great at keeping secrets.

He opens his mouth to speak, and I open mine to interject so I don't hear it. But his name spills from his perfect lips so smoothly that I have to stop myself—I just have to hear it.

"My name is Castiel King."

"Castiel…" I whisper in awe at the sound of it.

Castiel, Castiel, Castiel.

I say it over and over again in my mind, committing it to memory. I break apart the sounds, letting my eyes drift shut as my heart beats in time to match the cadence of it.

"Castiel." I open my eyes just as he brushes his lips over mine, the delicate touch such a stark contrast to his power.

He gently nips at my bottom lip, running his tongue across it, tasting me, forcing an uncharacteristically weak little whimper from my throat.

"I like your name," I whisper against his lips.

"Utter it to a single soul and you'll never utter another word again."

I stick out my tongue and lick from the bottom of his plump lower lip to the small dimple at the top of his upper lip. "I promise. Cross my heart, hope to die—"

Our mouths collide in a fury as he pushes forward against my lips, forcing them to part so he can taste me with his tongue. There's a primal growl from the back of his throat that he feeds me through this kiss, and it vibrates against my lips. The tremor shakes loose the lust he sparks and spreads it across my skin until every inch of me is prickling, tingling, and warm.

And then, without warning, he pulls away and stands. It takes me a few seconds to process his absence. I lean back, letting my head fall against the hard wood as I work to catch my breath.

I blink up at him, swallowing my anxiety at the fierce look in his eyes. "What are you going to do with me, Castiel?"

He flinches, as if he's not used to hearing his name, as if it affects him. It *must* affect him to hear it if no one else knows who he is… if I'm the only one who knows his name.

Fuck.

I'm the only one who knows the name of the Deity.

I can't even clamp my thighs shut to hide the slickness soaking my panties.

He doesn't respond, just stares down at me with those dark, brooding eyes. His thick eyebrows are straight, no expression of anger or confusion, and I would hardly know he's fucking horny if it weren't for the way he pants, if it weren't for the way his cock presses thickly against his jeans. He reaches down and unbuckles his black leather belt, eyes never leaving me as he unhooks it and tugs, freeing it from the loops with a long, intentional drag.

My palms start to sweat as he folds the belt in his

hands, looping it to make it shorter, smacking his palm with the end of it.

"Well, fuck me six ways from Sunday."

A smirk touches his cheek and my, oh my, he could beat me to death right now, and I don't think I'd even care. Self-preservation is lost on me with this dangerous, dominant man.

I want him.

I want all of him.

I want to take whatever he'll give me.

He steps forward, reaches out with the belt firmly in hand, and flicks his wrist, smacking the inside of my thigh sharply with the looped belt. I let out a moan as my body tenses against the ache. I can't rub my hand over it, can't close my legs, can't pull away or twist or turn or fucking *move*. He smacks me again in the same spot, and I yelp. The sting spreads from the site of impact, pouring out through my skin, heating me, turning to desire as the heat ripples toward my cunt.

He strikes again… again… again… all in the same damn spot. I squirm, thigh muscles twitching, ankles kicking. My hands grip the chains above the cuffs that hold my wrists, and my hips shift forward on the chair. I'm sinking, losing myself to sensation, losing myself to his rule.

Fuck, he's powerful.

He hits my thighs, my knees, my arms, even my fucking fingers until I'm an aching, writhing mess.

I equally love it and hate it.

I want him to stop, but I want more.

My breath catches when he grabs the front of my corset between my breasts and tugs it down sharply, exposing me.

"Shit!" I arch my back, trying to adjust myself against the boning that digs into my stomach and presses upward beneath my tits.

He positions himself beside me, and I know what he's about to do.

Do it.

Don't do it.

Fucking do it!

He strikes flat across my nipple. My back arches and I hiss, but I don't even have time to worry about the pain. He bends unexpectedly, cupping my breast in one hand and clamping his mouth around the bud.

I moan as his tongue swipes across my nipple, tasting me before sucking me into his mouth. He sucks rhythmically, drawing out my ability to think, to speak, to do anything other than sink in pleasure. My body slumps in the chair, my ass slipping closer to the edge, though not by much with my legs strapped in place.

I feel everything.

I feel the clenching need in my stomach. I feel my muscles tense and twitch as I writhe, trying to move closer to him, trying to move away from him, trying to keep still. I feel the rigid wood against the back of my head, against my neck, practically flattening my ass. I feel the hard edges of the wooden armrest cut into my flesh when I try to pull my legs back unsuccessfully.

My head rolls back and forth as his empty hand reaches between my legs, fingers wiggling as they brush over my covered pussy. "Oh, my fucking *God*."

I chuckle at my own words. He is actually the fucking self-proclaimed Deity. Every orgasm I've ever had in the Tower I've credited to him in my screaming. All the, "*Oh, God, oh, Gods,*" were just a plea to him, a fucking prayer for the almighty Deity himself to touch me, to show me what it feels like to come at the hands of a god.

He rubs three fingers over my panties and fishnets, rubbing right along my slit and pressing in on the fabric. I hear him groan and my head rolls toward him.

Something's happening here and I don't know exactly what, but he looks a little… lost. Not like, "*I've never had sex with a girl, and I can't find her clit,*" kind of lost. That would be fucking sad for a man like Castiel. He looks lost, like he's getting off on this but he didn't intend to. Though I have no idea what else his intentions would be in strapping me to a chair like this.

His wavy hair falls across his eyes, his lips part with his panting breaths, and his eyes hood. He bends and his forehead falls to mine as he wiggles his fingers into one of the holes in the fishnets, sweeps them beneath my panties, and teases along my pussy. My gut sinks and my body coils toward my belly, though I don't move much, locked in place the way I am.

His nose nudges mine, rubs across my cheek covered in dried blood, inhales my scent as it draws a line along my jaw. With my head turned toward him, I seek his lips, kissing his rough, dark almost-beard, letting it scratch my lips as we descend into gasping, writhing shells of human beings.

"Castiel," I whisper, pleading. "Hurt me, fuck me, make me come."

I nearly scream as he shoves three thick fingers inside me, and fuck, I'm glad I'm so wet because they are *thick*. He separates them inside me, stretching my walls, twisting his hand so they turn and brush along every inch inside.

It almost hurts.

It's almost painful.

But that line is so blurred that I can't tell where the pain ends and the pleasure begins. He starts to thrust his hand, stabbing into me with his stretched-out fingers over and over and over again.

"Does it feel good, baby doll? Does it make you want me?"

"Yes, I want you. I want you, Castiel."

He groans, nipping at my jawline as he removes his ring finger, turns his palm upward and rubs my g-spot expertly with two fingers still inside me.

I gasp, whimper, try to push down harder on his hand, but my ass is down as far as my strapped legs will allow. I grip the chains tighter, pull as hard as I can to lift my ass from the seat, just a little, just so I can thrust toward him.

"Fuck," he hisses, his cheek pressed to mine as we both look down at his hand, watching where his knuckles disappear inside me.

"Please. Please, please, *please*," I beg with pouting lips. "Lover... *please*."

His thumb joins in on the beautiful assault, rubbing my clit as he strokes inside me, driving me close, close, closer to the edge.

I'm lost now.

Out of my mind.

Gasping, twisting, writhing, fucking... a hot mess of lust that's merely a slave to his hand.

The hand of a fucking god.

I'm almost there. I swear, I'm gonna come so hard all over his hand—it's gonna be a mess.

I want it. I need it.

I'm almost there.

God...

Shit...

Fuck...

His hand disappears, and he steps back.

I jerk upright. "No..." I whine like a sad little girl because that's how I feel. I had a fucking lollipop in my hand... I was just about to lick it, and he ripped it away from me. "Please. Why did you stop?"

He roughly pushes his fingers against my pouting lips, forcing them apart, shoving his fingers inside my mouth. "Suck."

I hollow out my cheeks to suck on his soaked fingers, tasting myself on him. He shoves deeper, nearly making me gag, and then he pulls them out, my lips popping around them as they come out with a snap.

He moves back and lets out a heavy breath. A twisted smile forms on his face and it makes my clit fucking angry. "Time to get some sleep, baby doll. You've had a big day."

I laugh and it morphs into a dark chuckle. "You fucker. Hell no. You be a man of your word and finish what you fucking started."

"I don't believe I made you any promises."

"Your thumb on my clit made the promises, lover."

He shrugs. "You be a good girl now, Tempest. Get some sleep and we'll see if my thumb wants more of your clit in the morning." He strips and walks into his bathroom, turning on the shower.

"You motherfucker!" I yell after him, twisting uselessly in my binds.

That *asshole*.

I can't even finish myself off.

I throw my head back against the hard wood and laugh, cackling like a maniac. His touch was so good… so, *so* good. Better than anything I've ever felt before. He gave it to me, just to take it away, and I could nearly cry.

That's a fucking feeling right there.

I want more, so much more with that man.

If playing his game is the only way to earn his trust and get more from him, then I'll play.

Oh, I'll play.

And before long, we'll be playing together.

That man is a god, a king, a spiritual fucking catharsis—he's everything I never knew I needed, but I do need him.

I've managed to calm my breaths to something resembling normalcy by the time he's finished his shower and returned from the bathroom. I thought I had my pulsing pussy under control, but damn if that girl doesn't have a mind of her own.

He has a towel around his waist and his perfect, tan skin is still covered in droplets from the shower. The water glistens over rippling ab muscles that look absolutely unreal. I force my eyes up to meet his, connecting with his gaze—definitely not looking at his dampened chocolate hair as he tosses it with a small hand towel.

"Are you gonna be a good girl?" he asks with a tilt of his head.

I sigh. "Yes."

"Good." He nods once, drops his towel, and crosses the room.

I whimper and sink at the sight of his cock, but I don't utter a single word. I won't give him that satisfaction—not yet, at least. He flicks off the light and shrouds us in overwhelming darkness. I blink, but the room is pitch-black, with no windows, just darkness. I hear him move, hear him climb into the bed and settle on the mattress.

Fuck, fuck, fuck.

He's gonna leave me strung up like this all night. I'm suddenly very aware of how uncomfortable this position is, how it will creep toward painful before the night ends.

How am I supposed to get any sleep?

"Are you seriously gonna leave me like this?"

There's a long pause, silence between us before he finally says, "Yes."

Okay.

All right.

I can do this.

I've got this.

In minutes, I hear soft snoring and I wish I could untie my boots, just so I could fling one across the room at him. I slump and resign myself to accept that I'm going to have a seriously bad night.

CHAPTER SIX
you earned it

I MEWL IN disappointment as my mind drifts from sleep to awareness. I don't want to be aware; I don't want to be awake. I'm in so much pain in this stupid chair that at one point, I actually started crying. I cried and begged for minutes, but Castiel didn't come. That was probably—hopefully—hours ago.

I don't want to wake up in this chair again.

I want to stay asleep.

But life is slowly returning to my sleeping limbs. My legs—which had prickled until they were numb—are tingling now, blood flow returning to wake my aching muscles.

It's still dark in the room as I blink. I'm about to whine, maybe cry again about being awake, when I realize that firm, but tender hands are kneading my legs, from my ankles, over my shins and the sides of my calves, over my knees, up my thighs.

It feels amazing.

I sigh, a moan of appreciation slipping out.

I feel the movement as he brings his hands to my left foot, untying the laces of my black boots. I nearly come when he pulls the shoe off and drops it to the floor. I don't even care that my feet have been sweating in those heavy boots for hours when his hands grip my foot and squeeze, thumbs pressing in and rubbing circles on the bottom of my arch.

His hands creep upward, gliding over my shin, and I feel him tug the strap around my leg. He unbuckles the strap, the metal buckle clanging against the wooden seat as it falls away before he drops the strap to the ground. Tenderly, he lowers my leg from the armrest, putting it down with care. He moves onto the other leg, repeating his motions—removing my boot, rubbing my foot, removing the strap, and letting my leg down.

I would slump from the chair and crumble into a ball at his feet if it weren't for the way my wrists were still bound beside my head. Sadly, I don't sense movement from him to remove that binding.

In the quiet darkness, I can hear his breathing. It's heavy and quick, but carefully controlled. My smart mouth itches to say something stupid, but somehow, I can't. I've never felt so effectively silenced by another person. But it's good; I feel heard without having to say a word.

His hands clamp down on my thighs and squeeze. I moan at the sensation over sore muscles. His hands push upward and quickly slip behind me, grabbing my ass and dragging my body closer to the edge of the seat. The movement stretches my back, and fuck, that feels good. But it doesn't feel nearly as good as Castiel's fingers, grappling in the dark to slip along my belly, gripping the miniskirt, my panties, and the top of my fishnet stockings before gradually pulling them off.

He pulls the clothing free from my body until my bottom half is bare, the black corset still cinched uncomfortably around my waist. As my legs tingle and prickle with the blood flow returning to my muscles, he lifts them up and puts them over his strong shoulders.

"I need you to get wet for me, baby doll."

Baby doll.

I fucking love how that sounds.

He inhales my scent as his lips brush across my inner thigh, moving closer and closer to my pussy. Then, all at once, his mouth is on me, tongue licking all the way along my slit, flicking over my clit.

I whimper.

"Are you gonna be a good girl?"

"Yes," my voice is a breathy moan, "I'll be good for you."

"I'm the only one you need to be good for."

Lips, tongue, teeth, his scratchy beard, the tip of his nose; all of it attacks my pussy, and I think I've died and gone to heaven.

Well, I suppose I have, haven't I?

The Deity himself is rewarding me with pleasure in his heavenly penthouse. He's on his knees for me, tasting me, swirling his tongue, making me wet… And *shit*, I feel powerful. There's something so empowering about having a man's face between your thighs—especially if that man is motherfucking Castiel King.

I might just be in love if there is such a thing.

It doesn't take long before I'm dripping for him, wetness flowing from the way he sucks on my clit. His ferocious pace gradually slows, and I worry he's going to stop, fake me out again like he did last time.

He pulls away and I protest, "No, please."

"You don't need to beg."

I feel his body move around me, his presence like a light I could track, even in the dark. Still, it startles me when I feel his hands suddenly on my wrists. I sigh when he removes the cuff from my left wrist, and I drop my hand. It feels weird, the limb slowly tingling back to life.

He moves around me and soon, the right wrist is freed, too. My body feels weak and limp. I'm turned-on but unable to move, so lax from my sore muscles and lack of sleep.

He moves in front of me, bending over and leaning in close. He grabs my arms and puts them around his neck.

"Hang on."

I fold my arms around him, fingers still prickling and my grip unsure. Then his hands move to my thighs, and he wraps my legs around his waist. I gasp when I feel his hard cock rub against me. I somehow manage to lock my legs around his hips as his hands slip to my ass, and he plucks me from the chair with ease. I'm afraid I'll fall because my muscles are twitching and tired, but his hold on me is firm.

He moves a couple of steps backward, then lowers to sit on the edge of the bed. My legs touch the soft comforter and I moan, the thought of laying down and falling asleep beneath it so enticing.

But there's something even more enticing, and he quickly draws my attention to it. He reaches behind him to grip my ankles, twisting and pulling my legs back until I'm positioned with my knees on the bed, straddling his lap. I can feel his massive hard-on slide against my cunt and suddenly, sleep doesn't concern me.

"Make yourself come, baby doll. You earned it."

Holy fucking hell.

What is this feeling washing over me?

It's like relief, but it's tinged with pride.

It's like lust, but filled with emotion.

It's like a constant need, but one that has already been fulfilled.

His hand moves to my lower back and presses me closer, encouraging me to arch my back. It's not like he needs to encourage it. I feel him like gravity without a single touch, drawing me in, demanding my attention, making me want to please him when all I've ever wanted was to please myself and fucking survive.

Who is this man?

I let my body slump and his cock easily slips inside me. He's so thick—if I weren't already wet for him, it would probably hurt—and he fills me so completely that there's no room for emptiness. His arms wrap around me and hold me against him, and I'm thankful for it. I can hardly hold myself upright, but I want that goddamn orgasm and I'm gonna chase it. All I have to do is rock my hips. He's at the perfect angle to rub against all the right spots.

I sink all the way down, letting my clit grind against the base of his cock. He kisses my neck, just behind my ear, and runs his nails down my back, the sensation surprising me. I roll my hips back and forth, grinding with him buried deep, and it doesn't take me long to get to that desperate edge.

"Let me come," I breathe against his ear before I lick the side of his face from jaw to hairline. "Please, let me come."

He already said I could, so why the fuck am I asking?

Why does he make me want to ask?

One hand creeps up, fingers combing into my hair at the base of my skull. He grips my head and wrenches it back. If it weren't dark, I know I'd be meeting his eyes right now.

He holds my head still as he kisses me deeply, his tongue diving inside my mouth, feeding me passion. After a few breathless moments, he breaks the kiss and presses his forehead to mine. "You're my good girl, aren't you?"

I nod against his forehead. "For you."

Shit, I'm not even lying.

I wanna be good for him, whatever that even means.

"Come, Tempest. Do it now."

As if on command, I peak, my hips fiercely grinding back and forth. It sparks in my clit and ignites my senses, exploding pleasure from my clenching pussy, but it doesn't end there like it usually does. It spreads, rippling out in waves through my entire body. It's so intense that I can feel it in my fucking eyeballs. My body is literally trembling out of control as I ride the shattering orgasm, as it rips through me and breaks me apart.

Before it's over, I'm on my back, my ass down at the edge of the bed, and Castiel between my legs. He holds my left knee against his hip, his other hand gripping my waist with painful, prodding fingertips. He groans as he fucks me *hard*—harder than I've ever been fucked before. It's just skin slapping against skin and moaning and groaning from both of us as he fucks me in the dark.

After being in that goddamn chair, after the ache in my muscles and the release of that powerful orgasm, I'd be content to lie right here forever and let him fuck me until I die.

I feel him swelling just before the release, feel him grow thicker just before he groans and spills inside me. And then he folds over me, still buried, laying his body on top of mine, and searching for my lips.

His short beard scratches and his tongue soothes as he seeks my mouth, running up my neck and along my cheek. When his lips touch mine, I reach up, dig my fingers into his silky, soft hair, and pull him down against my face. We consume each other until there's nothing left of us as individuals, until we're just one damaged soul chasing redemption in our violent world.

As the high falls and we come back into our bodies, as the aches and pains return to my previously stretched and bound muscles, I'm surprised to find that I still feel good, still feel somehow connected—and not just because his cock is still inside me.

His face nuzzles into my neck. "You're mine now. Do you understand that, baby doll? You belong to me."

I nod, not entirely sure I understand, but willing to accept it for orgasms like that… and for personal safety. Not necessarily in that order.

Okay, probably in that order.

"Say it," he urges. "Tell me who you belong to."

"I belong to you, lover."

"Good." His fingers find my chin and pinch my jaw, holding my head still. "And don't you fucking forget it."

CHAPTER SEVEN
don't call me lover

"I DON'T UNDERSTAND," I say to Castiel, who's standing somewhere behind me in my bedroom on the twentieth floor.

I stare down at the outfit laid out on my bed—white lace bralette, matching panties, white silk robe, and silver jewelry.

"What don't you understand?"

I glance over my shoulder at him, fresh from the shower in all my naked glory. He's brooding, arms folded over his chest, stance wide and domineering as he impatiently waits for me to dress.

"I thought I belonged to you now. But you're sending me to work as an angel tonight?"

"You're an alter; you've always belonged to me."

"After last night, I thought—"

"It's stupid to make assumptions, Tempest."

My chest rises with a heavy, indignant breath. "Fine. So last night was nothing. Just punishment and fucking."

It was so not *just punishment and fucking.*

I don't know what it was, but I know it was more than that.

He clears his throat, breaking character in a way that makes a secret smile creep up my lips as I reach for the panties. "Right," he says.

"Right," I repeat, quickly pulling on the underwear. "So, you're gonna watch me fuck a winning player tonight. How do you feel about that, lover?"

"I feel like you're gonna be late if you don't shut up and get dressed."

I grab the bralette and spin around to face him, dangling the skimpy fabric by its thin strap on my pointer finger. "I'd hardly call this getting dressed."

"Put it on."

"You sure you really want me to be an angel tonight?" I stride across the room toward him, pushing my hips through an intentional sway. "We could just stay here... I could be *your* angel, lover."

I watch his throat bob as he swallows, his eyes darting down to my bare tits. I internally cheer for that small victory, that small slip in his carefully controlled demeanor. Deciding to press my luck, I step closer and he drops his arms to his sides. I lean into him, molding my body to his, standing up on my toes to reach his lips. I kiss the corner of his mouth, then sneak out my tongue and lick a flat line up the side of his cheek to claim him.

He catches me off-guard as his head whips to the side. He bares his teeth and snaps them down on my tongue, biting into flesh. I squeal and jump back, rolling my tongue around in my mouth against the sharp and bruising pain.

"Get dressed," he commands, and I see in his eyes how he actively works to shield himself.

He feels something.

I know he does.

He may be god-like, but he is human in the flesh, and all humans feel. Some of them feel bad things and some of them good, but everyone *feels*. Castiel feels *something* toward me, and whether it's a good something or a bad something, it's there. It's at least enough feeling to make him want to hurt me and fuck me.

I put on the bralette to cover my breasts, though you could hardly call it coverage since you can still see my nipples through the meager lace fabric. I grab the silver layered necklace and unclasp the hook. The shortest layer will fit tightly around my neck, like a choker. I could put it on myself, but I feign incompetency and hold it up to Castiel.

"Will you help me put this on?"

He hesitates, but then strides forward, grabbing it from

my hand. I gather my hair and pull it over one shoulder before he wraps the necklace around my throat. I feel his fingertips brush over my skin as he clasps it in the back.

Once it's hooked, he gives it a slight tug from the back, tightening it around my throat for just a moment before letting go and stepping back. I look down at the charm dangling from the choker above the two longer layers of the necklace—one of which lays flat against my chest, the other stopping just above the bralette.

The charm is a silver crescent, though I wouldn't call it a half-moon. I would call it a C—*for Castiel*—but I don't know whether I'm hopefully longing for his claim or naïvely grasping at straws.

"You really want me to be your girl, huh?" I turn to face him as a cheeky smile stretches across my face. I playfully tilt my head, twisting my fingers to highlight the charm resting against my throat. "C for Castiel? You can brand me if you want to. I might like it."

"It's a crescent moon. Don't fool yourself, Tempest."

I let go of the charm and grab the short silk robe from the bed, quickly slipping it on over my shoulders. I move in close to his body and look up at him. "I'm not fooling myself, lover. I know I'm under your skin, seeping into your veins, poisoning your blood. Last night was different for you, wasn't it? Have you fucked any of your alters before?"

"That's none of your business."

"You haven't, have you?"

His hand shoots out in a flash and wraps around my throat, the silver C digging into both of our flesh, connecting my throat and his palm. "Why do you insist on challenging a god?"

"Why do you enjoy it so much?"

He bends over me, arching me backward, but holding me firmly in his grip. My hands come up to grab his wrist and forearm, holding on, because if he lets go, I'm going to fall backward. He turns his head, swipes his tongue sideways across my mouth, then bites my bottom lip—it's more of a nibble than a bite, but it has me wanting him instantly.

"You have a job to do tonight. Quit making more of this than it is."

"Well, what is it, then?" I blink up at him with mock innocent eyes. "I thought I was your baby doll."

His breath is hot against my cheek as he moves in closer, his lips brushing the shell of my ear. "You *are* my baby doll. A pretty little plaything to dress-up and fuck with and *use.* Don't read into it."

I pull my head back and give him my eyes. "Don't give me something to read into and I won't. Your eyes don't lie, lover."

"Don't call me *lover.*"

"*Lover.*"

His jaw twitches, teeth grinding behind his closed lips. He stares at me with an intensity that reminds me he could kill me and no one would care. He could strangle me with that one strong hand around my throat, and there would be no consequences for him, not in this world. But I don't think he wants to. Because if he really wanted me gone—if he really wanted me dead—he would've done it as soon as he found out about *Tempest in the Tower*.

I have to do it.

I have to say it.

I have to push him, just a little more, just to see what he'll do.

"Kill me, lover. Strangle me, break my neck. If I'm really just a rag doll for you to play with, then making me work means nothing to you. You don't need me to be an alter. You don't need me to go fuck this winning player because of some stupid rules you came up with for the Tower. End me. Fucking *kill* me."

In one fell swoop, he whips me around, grabs the back of my head, and shoves my face down on the bed. He grabs my panties and tugs them down, dragging them to my thighs. I gasp, suddenly breathless. He really has a way of taking my breath away.

Shit. Did I just seduce him into wanting to take my breath away for real?

He smacks my ass hard, with a heavy, bruising hand, before cupping my pussy.

"Tempt me," he says. "Go on. Tell me to kill you one more fucking time."

I press up onto my elbows as his palm squeezes over my

sex, the heel of his hand digging against my opening. I turn my head over my shoulder to look at him. "Kill me."

His hand shifts as he grunts with thick desire. Without any warning at all, he wedges four fingers against my slick entrance. I squeal as his nails graze skin, scratching carelessly as he twists his way inside me. He wiggles his hand, pressing hard, working nearly his entire fist inside me.

"Fuck!" I gasp, not sure if it's painful or pleasurable, thankful that he already had me turned-on and wet by his very presence before this exchange even started.

"Does that hurt, baby doll?"

"Shit. Yes… no."

"Which is it?"

"No?"

"How about now?" He sinks in past the knuckles and rotates his hand.

Fuck, that hurts!

"It's *so* good, lover," I lie. "Why don't you shove your fist inside me?"

He chuckles and my stomach clenches, sending a rush of wetness over his fingers. I don't know how the fuck he manages to turn me on so much when he's hurting me. "Fuck, you're so wet."

My words are quiet, breathy. "That's all for you, lover."

He rips his hand away, and I moan sadly at the sudden absence, mourning the loss of the sinful way he stretched me past my limit.

"Save it for the player," he says with an edge to his voice. He's trying to sound mean, but it doesn't come off quite as intended. I can hear the break in his gruff tone as he marches off to the bathroom. I hear the faucet turn on and can guess he's washing his hand.

"I would've licked it off for you!" I shout after him.

I stand and pull my panties back on, blowing out a breath to steady myself and my suddenly weak knees. A moment later, the faucet shuts off and he returns, but he doesn't look at me. He just strides toward the door and wrenches it open with a harsh yank.

"Let's go."

"Fine." I march past him and make sure it's obvious when I scratch the side of my forehead with my middle finger.

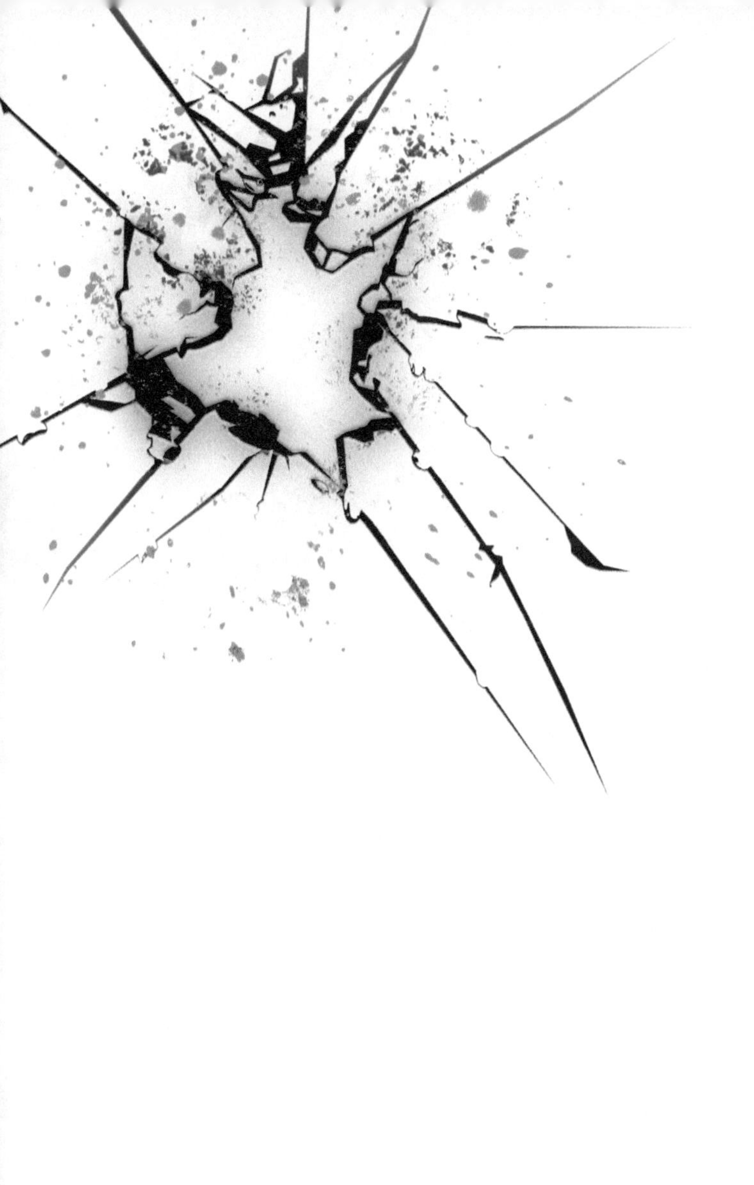

CHAPTER EIGHT

oops

WE TAKE THE elevator to the seventh floor and the metal doors open to Heaven. Much like Castiel's penthouse, this floor is perfect and pristine and white. The hallway is lined on either side with gold-framed mirrors hung on the white walls. A crystal chandelier hangs from the center, bouncing light off the reflections of the mirrors to create an ethereal glow. The floors are covered in a plush, white carpet that absorbs the sound of my white stilettos as we pad across it.

My energy climbs as Castiel leads me forward, passing one door after the other. The closer we come to the end of the hallway, the more excited I get. The last room on the left is the White Room—my favorite room—with the perfect city view out from the picture window. When he reaches for the handle of the White Room, my excitement peaks and

I'm practically bouncing to go inside.

He pushes the door open and holds it as I move past the threshold into the room. I go straight to the window before doing anything else. I hear the door click shut as I put my hands on the glass and press my forehead to it.

"Fuck, I love this view."

It's quiet for a few moments before he speaks. "Why?"

"Why?" My forehead wrinkles, crinkling against the glass. "Just look. There's a whole world out there."

"A brutal one."

"Yeah, but it wasn't always that way." I move my fingertip along the glass, pointing toward a space of trash-covered, grassy lawn in the distance. "That used to be a park. I remember my brother pushing me on the swings there when I was little. He was five years older than me, so our parents let us go by ourselves sometimes. We felt so fucking cool."

I feel Castiel approach, like the pulsing thrum of dark matter creeping into my energy field. "Where's your brother now?" he asks once he's at my back. I can see his reflection just behind me in the glass, his eyes looking down at the back of my head as he takes in breath after heavy breath.

"Dead."

"The Syndicate," he confirms. It's not a question; he knows.

Everybody knows.

Everybody has lost someone to the Syndicate's violence.

"He's dead because of me."

I see his reflected head tilt slightly to the side as his dark eyebrows furrow. "How?"

"Do you really want to know?" I suddenly feel tense. I don't want to think about this. I don't want to talk about this, especially not before servicing some asshole's fantasies as an angel.

He bends and his nose brushes through my hair at the back of my head. I take in a sharp breath and hold it, unable to move as he inhales deeply, taking in the scent of me. His hands find my waist as his body falls against mine, pressing me to the glass.

"Tell me."

"It's not a very compelling story."

"*Tell me.*"

"You're so fucking pushy."

"I thought you were gonna be a good girl for me, baby doll."

Well, shit.

That shouldn't have any effect on me; I shouldn't give a shit about being a good girl for him, especially when he's such an asshole to me. But I *do* give a shit. It's something about the way he touches me that zaps my will to resist and makes me want to open up to him and give him whatever he asks for.

My lips start moving before my brain can decide to clam up and keep my mouth shut. "It happened when we were walking home after getting our food rations."

The words kick up my anxiety, bringing me back to the events of that day, wanting to pull me into a nervous, stress-filled loop. But then his fingers find my hair and brush it back over my shoulder. His hand slides into the crook of my neck and he gently lays his fingers over my collarbone, stroking softly over my skin. Somehow it makes me feel stronger to be at his mercy.

"It was three years after the takeover. I was thirteen, he was eighteen. We took the same path home we always took, through back-alleys, staying close to the buildings, hidden and quick. It was rare we encountered anyone on the path we'd carefully mapped, but when we did, it was usually other citizens just trying to make their way home, too. That day, though, we encountered three Syndicate leaders. They saw him, an eighteen-year-old potential recruit, and they saw me..."

"A pretty thirteen-year-old girl."

I spin suddenly in his hold, pushing my back to the glass, my natural defensive sarcasm popping out from my lips. "Aw, you think I'm pretty?"

"Stop." He calls me out on my shit. "Tell me what happened."

I swallow the dry lump rising in my throat. "The same thing that happens to every little girl found wandering in the city." I hold his gaze with mine. "They told me if I was a good girl they'd let us both live, that they'd take my brother to work for them and let me leave with my life. All I had to do was get on my knees and open my pretty little mouth for them."

The air rushes from his lungs as he exhales heavily, washing his warmth over me. He reaches up to brush a strand of my purple hair from my face and his touch electrifies my skin, like a lightning bolt of strength and power that only a touch from a god could give.

"I did what they told me to do. I played by their rules and sucked them all off beside a dumpster in the alleyway. And you know what it got me? An aching jaw, cum on my face, a black eye, and a dead brother. Because they killed him anyway. They made him watch it all happen, and then they killed him.

"And you know what? It's my own fucking fault. I shouldn't have followed their rules. I should have known they couldn't be trusted. I should have done what my brother always told me I should do if we were ever to encounter them. I should have ran… but I didn't. If they weren't so high off their own power and looking to get a kick out of torturing me, they might've let him live. Recruited him for defense or border security or some shit. But I was too fucking scared to run, and it got us both hurt in the end."

Castiel's expressionless face isn't so expressionless in the moment—it's almost understanding, perhaps even sympathetic. He cups my cheek in his palm and leans in close, laying his forehead on mine. "It's not your fault, baby doll."

I shrug a shoulder. "It doesn't matter anymore."

"You're safe here in the Tower."

I laugh a little at that. "Am I? Am I safe with you, lover?"

He shocks me with a gentle kiss, so soft and tender that it makes my heart beat faster. "Yes. It's why I built this business in the aftermath."

I incline my head, kissing the corner of his mouth. "Why do they leave you alone? Why do they let you operate? Why are we untouchable here as alters?"

"You're asking me to tell you my secrets, *Tempest in the Tower*."

"*Tempest in the Tower* is gone. You killed her, smashed her phone. It's just a baby doll asking her lover."

His eyes are locked on mine, digging in, burrowing deep, twisting and shoveling their way into my soul—and I don't dare look away.

I hold him there in my stare until he sighs and his shoulders slump. "I agreed to help them manage the population in exchange for certain freedoms. The system was their design, in keeping with the tone of the new city they wanted to create—violent, cruel, unpredictable. They knew they could lure people in with gambling and promises of extra rations or the possibility of winning the company of a beautiful woman. But it's just another system of control, Tempest. No one ever really wins here. Nine out of the ten men you play angel for will end up back here, losing big. You see them again in the Hellscape. No citizen ever really gets more than their fair share of rations. Control is the reason why there are alters. It's why you play demon. To *control*."

I put my hands on his chest and shove him back, my eyebrows furrowing as unexpected anger takes over.

We're all just pawns in the Syndicate's sick game?

I feel fucking deceived. I feel like I've been tricked into playing this game for the promise of safety as an alter.

But I don't have any right to be angry.

I knew I'd be killing people when I took on this job. If that doesn't make me just as low and filthy as the Syndicate, then I don't know what else would. That doesn't stop me from feeling indignation at learning that I'm just a pawn. I open my mouth to tell Castiel just how angry I am, but we're interrupted by the click of the opening door. Castiel releases me and backs away, walking to the door as one of the authority graciously ushers in a winning player.

I can't believe he's making me do this after last night.

I'm so fucking pissed off right now, I could scream. But it doesn't matter. I don't get to be pissed off now, not when I have my fucking job to do. I have to play my part. I push off the glass, smooth my hair, and stride across the room to greet the winning player just as the authority leaves, closing the door behind him.

Castiel stands beside it, watching me expectantly, anxiously…

What the fuck is that look?

I refuse to give him my eyes because, right now, I'm angry at who he is and what he does. I don't know why I wasn't so angry about it before. I knew from the beginning what it meant to be an alter, and knowingly signed up. I understood that I'd be murdering people in the name of playing by someone else's rules—the unknown Deity's rules.

But I never really had a choice.

It was kill or be killed, and I chose selfishly. If I had to choose all over again, I'd make the same choice, though it felt different when I thought it was just a safe place for me to work a creepy job than it does now that I know *why* I play demon.

Castiel's just a pawn in their game, too. How can I be angry with him for this?

I lift my chin, pull my shoulders back, and push out my tits as I approach the player. This one is reasonably attractive, which is a nice change of pace for me. Perfectly styled blond hair, sharp blue eyes, square jaw, toned frame, and slim build. I'm a little thrown off by his appearance because he looks awfully put-together for a gambling player.

"Hi, handsome." I bat my eyelashes. "I'll be your angel tonight. Welcome to the White Room. Can I get you something to drink before we begin?"

A half-smile creeps up the side of his cheek, and he shakes his head. "No, I'm good. Why don't we just get started, beautiful?"

"Of course." I give Castiel a sideways glance as he backs up to the wall behind him, shoving his hands inside his pockets and placing a booted foot up against the wall as he leans. I reach out and delicately take the player's hand in mine, turning toward the bed and walking toward it, pulling him behind me. I gracefully sit on the edge and pat the spot just beside me. He sits down next to me, our hips touching. "What should I call you tonight?"

"You want my name?"

"It doesn't have to be your name if you don't want." I lean in close and pretend to pick lint from his collar, just so I can move into his space because I'm a motherfucking professional and I know what I'm doing. I look up at Castiel across the room, and I can see his shoulders twitch. It makes me smile. "I can call you anything you want me to, baby."

With a sudden movement, the player reaches out, wraps his palm around a chunk of my hair, and yanks my head back, forcing my chin to rise toward the ceiling. He bends to my neck and boldly licks from the hollow of my throat to the bottom of my chin before brushing his nose along the curve of my neck. "Why don't you call me... daddy."

Yeah, okay.

My cheeks twitch and a laugh threatens to climb its way up my throat, but I force myself to play it cool. I see movement from the corner of my eye and glance over to take a peek at Castiel just as he throws his arms across his puffed-out chest. He's agitated, annoyed with having to watch this exchange.

But is he amused?

I wish he'd show some hint on his deadpan face. As angry as I am with him, I feel like this whole thing would be easier if I could secretly share my amusement with him, because this is fucking funny.

Okay, Tempest.

Think serious.

Think sexy.

"Of course… *daddy*." The player releases my hair and strokes his hand down my back slowly, stopping when his hand hits the mattress. "Tell me, daddy. How can I serve your fantasies tonight?"

"For starters, you can get down on your knees where you belong, you fucking whore."

Okay, okay, easy there, killer.

He's not the first winning player to demean me, talk down to me, getting his rocks off on humiliation and rough sex. Men like to have power, and when they don't have it, they forget how to behave like respectable human beings. The Syndicate stole power from a lot of men in the takeover and unfortunately, that leaves us with a lot of disrespectful, power-hungry, whiny men crawling the city streets.

But whatever, it's just a part of the job.

With a subtle sigh, I slip off the bed and onto my knees in front of him. Raising up, I put my hands on his thighs, leaning forward, squeezing my breasts together with my upper arms as I slowly push my palms toward his belt.

"Are you gonna put me in my place, daddy?" I blink at him innocently.

"Take out my cock and suck it, bitch."

Geez, fuckboy, bring the charm down a few notches, huh?

I sigh but force a coy smile as I reach for his belt buckle. I've barely gotten it undone before he snatches me harshly by the chin. "Wipe the fucking smile off your face. This isn't meant to be fun for you."

I swallow, taking in a sharp breath through my nose. I hate guys like this; I *really* fucking hate them. Some of these players are happy just to spend time with a pretty girl like me. The old guys are better about that, mostly because they have a harder time getting it up… or maybe because they can't get it from anyone out there and they're lonely, just happy to have won my attention for an hour. But guys like this blond shithead remind me how brutal it really is out there.

"Yes, daddy," I mutter, hiding my sarcasm as I let a scowl replace my smile.

He grins at me, and it makes me wanna punch him in the balls. "That's better. I want you to fight me."

Ah, yes, the ever clever pretend-you-don't-want-it game.

He stands without warning, forcing me to sit back on my heels. He doesn't let go of my chin as he uses one hand to finish popping the button and pulling his zipper down. He shoves his pants and underwear down until his almost-hard dick pops free.

I really fucking hate this part.

I hate being on my knees for oral.

My fingers twitch at my sides and I drum them against my thighs, just to work out some of the anxious energy. I swallow hard as he shuffles forward.

"Open," he says.

"Open your mouth and lick it, little girl, or we'll kill your fucking brother. Go on now, be good. That's it now."

I squeeze my eyes shut tight to force out the awful memory. I clench my fists, letting my fingernails dig into my palms so I can focus on the sting rather than the memory.

I open my mouth wide and swallow hard to avoid gagging as he shoves his dick inside my mouth. He's not easy about it, reaching around to grip the back of my head as he pushes all the way in. I struggle against my gag reflex as he holds me in place, refusing to give me one second of relief to fucking *breathe*. And then, the stupid fucker pulses—he pulses his cock against the back of my throat until I'm gagging. Instinctively, I put my hands up against his thighs, trying to push him back, but he only pushes harder.

Shit.

I can't breathe.

I literally can't fucking *breathe*.

I'm coughing and spluttering, pushing and fighting, which is exactly what he wants, but *I* don't want it. I don't want this bullshit. It's just my job.

It's my motherfucking job.

And it's all for the goddamn Savage Syndicate!

I'm so angry that a scream forces its way from my throat, but the impact of it only gets caught on his suffocating dick.

And then everything is red.

Red, red, red.

I pinch my eyes shut as blood splashes across my face, as the player slips out from my mouth.

I swipe the back of my hands over my eyes as I cough and gasp. When I finally open my eyes, blinking slowly against the thick liquid coating my face, I see so much blood.

I see Castiel, and I see blood.

He's beside me, his chest rising and falling heavily as he stares down at the bleeding player who has fallen back on the bed, blood spurting from him in pulsing waves.

"What the *fuck?*"

Castiel turns his head to look down at me, his eyebrows furrowed in confusion, his dark eyes tinged with rage, his cheeks spattered with red. My eyes flicker down to see the knife in his hand—the one he pulled once before in his office on my former keeper from the strap around his calf.

I blink up at him in disbelief. "What did you do?"

His eyebrows slowly straighten as he watches me, his expression softening to his typical detachment. But it's not quite typical. There's a hint of humor in his smirk as he shrugs a shoulder and says, "Oops."

"Oops?" There's a quiet beat, and then I burst into

laughter. "*Oops?*" I sit back on my heels and laugh.

I look down at my white lingerie, my ivory skin, all covered in the winning player's thick, red blood. I slap a hand over my mouth to stop my cackling as unexpected tears replace the laughter.

Castiel crouches to his haunches beside me, studying my face carefully, watching tears drip down my cheeks. I tilt my head to the side. "Why did you do that?"

"I didn't like seeing you with another man." His face is still severe, serious, and deliberate. "I think you might be under my skin, baby doll." He hooks a finger beneath my chin and lifts gently, leaning in close and studying my eyes. "Are you okay?"

Quick check—heart pounding, pulse thrumming, chest tight, butterflies in my belly, stomach clenching, pussy suddenly and inexplicably wet with him in front of me...

Yeah, I'm good.

"Yes." I nod.

Unceremoniously, he pushes to his feet and flips the asshole over onto his stomach from where he fell on the bed. He reaches into his pocket and pulls out the guy's wallet, flipping through it as I slowly stand and shake the blood off my palms. I step forward, looking down at the man who fucked with me and lost. He lost because Castiel protected me.

He protected me.

I could nearly cry at the thought of it.

Instead, I spit on the man's back and flip him off with both hands.

Then my eyes land on something I never expected to see. And when I see it, my heart stops. When I see it, my hand jerks out to wrap around Castiel's wrist, but just for a moment. I quickly let go and climb on top of the dead man to get a closer look. Straddling his back, I swipe blood from the back of his neck and bend in close.

There, just beneath the end of his hairline, is a small, raised outline, the fresh wound of a healing tattoo. Two of the letter S, stacked on top of each other, the bottom S hooking through the top of the other in white ink.

We all know the mark—it's how we know who to trust out there in the city. Because only those who belong are allowed to wear their mark.

It's the mark of the Savage Syndicate.

CHAPTER NINE
big trouble

"OH, FUCK. WHAT have you done?" I turn my head to look over my shoulder at Castiel, and his eyes narrow at me.

"What?" The word is sharp, annoyed, curt in my questioning.

"Castiel… *look*." I reach back, grab his wrist, and tug. He's resistant, his eyebrows slanting in toward his nose at my boldness, but I only tug harder until he finally puts a knee up on the bed. "Look!" I point at the man's neck.

I watch his face as it slips from dominant resistance to outright horror. It's the loudest expression I've seen on this gorgeous man's face since I met him; and *fuck,* does it scare me.

He doesn't say anything as his eyes widen, as he combs his bloody fingers backward through his thick, dark hair. He covers his mouth with his hand and swipes down, unblinking, well and truly shocked at our current predicament.

"You killed someone from the Syndicate," I whisper, looking at him intently. "You killed someone from the Syndicate... for *me*."

"I didn't fucking know," he says.

I turn, moving on my knees in front of Castiel, gripping his face in my bloody hands. "You killed him for me." His chest is heaving, eyes still staring down at the white ink tattoo on the back of the dead player's neck. I scoot in closer, pressing my body against his, leaning in to press a soft kiss to his plump lips. "Lover, you killed him for *me*."

His eyes shift, meeting mine suddenly and with a burning intensity that makes goosebumps form on my arms.

"I killed him for you," he finally says, as if testing the words, unsure of their meaning, curious whether they're true or not. My heart hammers through the pause as his eyes flicker, cataloging every inch of my face. After what feels like hours of staring, hours of heated breath and tingling lips and gravity tugging between us, he finally speaks, and the words are filled with conviction. "I killed him for you."

Our lips collide with bruising force, and we wrap our arms around each other, squeezing, pulling, pushing, frantically trying to get closer. I want to seep inside him, melt and liquify and cover every inch of him like a crashing wave. His hands are in my hair, raking, gripping, tugging as he devours me with his kiss.

What the fuck is this?

What have we found here between us?

At some point—probably a century or two later—he breaks the kiss, rolling his forehead along mine and giving me full, unflinching eye contact. "We're in big trouble, baby doll."

"Big trouble, lover."

"No one can find out about this. Do you understand me?"

"About us?"

"No, baby, about the dead man from the fucking Syndicate beside you."

I have to glance over at him to remind myself because that kiss took away the whole damn world. "Oh, right. How the hell did he even get in here? Shouldn't the authority have caught him on the gambling floor?"

His eyes flash with anger. "Yes, they should have. They should've caught him coming in. They should have caught him placing a bet. They should have fucking caught him before bringing him to this fucking room and handing him over to an angel."

"Yeah, they really fucked up. But what do we do about it now?"

"We dispose of the body, and we pretend it never happened. I'll take care of the authority after. We need to get him down to the incinerator without alerting anyone's attention."

"If we can just get him to the service elevator, no one will be the wiser. It'll just look like he's a losing player being brought out from the Hellscape. We'll cut off his tattoo so the disposer won't have any chance of seeing it." I hold out my hand. "Give me the knife. I'll do it."

Without hesitation, he hands me his knife and my heart takes flight. The Deity—beautifully flawed Castiel King—hands me his knife without pause and it twists my insides pleasantly. It's a show of trust, something I never could have imagined he would show me.

I bend over the man, deciding that scratching up the skin with knicks and slices might make for better concealment than removing the patch of skin. I hack at the back of his neck deliberately as Castiel gets off the bed, heading for the door.

He comes back when I finish. I look down at my work and feel pleased that I've successfully managed to conceal the Savage Syndicate tattoo amidst bloody cuts and scratches.

"Go take a shower. I'll move the body."

"You can't move the body on your own. I'll help."

"Did I ask, Tempest? Go. Take. A shower. When I come back, you'd better be fucking pristine. I don't want a trace of blood on you."

"Let me help you—"

"No, baby doll. This is on me. Go."

I stare at him, surprised at how appreciative I feel for him handling this. He's taking care of this fucked up situation he put us in, but it's also like he's taking care of *me*. And that makes me feel like a goddamn princess.

"Okay, lover. But at least tell me I did a good job first." I wave my knife-wielding hand toward the dead player's back and Castiel glances at my hack job.

He leans over me, coming in close with all his heat that gets my heart pounding like crazy. "You did good." He gives me a quick peck on the lips, and I feel giddy—giddy like a little girl, and I love it.

I hop off the bed, practically skipping toward the attached bathroom, but stop mid-skip. "Oh." I turn and head back to him, holding out the knife. "Here you go." He takes it from me with a wink that makes me want to fuck him like crazy, but he returns the bloody knife to his calf holster and positions the body to lift it.

I'm frozen watching him crouch beside the bed, tugging on the man's arm to roll him to a sideways position. He hoists him over his shoulder and stands like it's nothing to deadlift a man's body.

Shit, that's hot.

Castiel is strong… like, freakishly fucking strong.

He spins with the man in his hold and his eyes fall on mine. "Stop soaking your panties watching me and get in the goddamn shower, Tempest."

I blink. I smile. I shrug. "Yes, lover," I whisper, then finally turn and head for the bathroom as he leaves the room with the dead man from the Savage Syndicate on his shoulders.

"FUCK, YES..." I moan, struggling to hold myself up on the edge of the wooden desk in Castiel's office.

The two spectacular views I have from this spot are literally making me wetter than I've ever been. The sun is setting and the light coming through the big picture window casts an orange glow across my body, making a striped pattern of shadow and light. But my view of the fading sunshine and the city isn't the best view in front of me.

It's the sight of Castiel's thick, wavy hair falling in sexy pieces over his dark eyes that really drives me crazy. Those dark eyes stare up at me from between my spread legs as he sucks on my clit with an aching rhythm that begs for release. He's been down there for the better part of an hour with no signs of slowing.

Heaven help me, this man is a sex god.

His hands grip my thighs, fingertips digging in with a bruising grip as he lets up on my clit to teasingly lick along my slit.

"Fuck, please, get back on my clit, lover. I'm so close."

"Shut up. You don't come until I'm ready to fuck you."

"Aren't you ready to fuck me yet?"

He stands suddenly, nearly knocking me onto my back, but I don't slip. He snakes an arm around my waist as his head dips to press his forehead to mine. I can see my wetness all over his perfect face, and I can't stop myself from licking, lapping, running my tongue all around his mouth to taste what he tastes when he eats me out. I put my mouth against his without kissing, just a gentle brush so he can feel my words. "Fuck me, lover. Make me come."

With a grunt and a heavy exhale, he kisses me with passion, gripping the back of my head with one hand as the other on my lower back drags me closer. I reach between us, unbuckling his belt, popping the button, pulling the zipper. My fingers scramble to free his cock, and I about die from anticipation as my palm wraps around it.

"Fucking take it," he commands against my mouth. "Put me inside you, baby doll."

I slide my ass forward on the desk, angle him toward me, and rub his tip against my folds. When he's right there, so close to being inside me, I let go, reach around him to grip his solid ass cheeks, and pull. He pushes inside me, filling me completely with one heavy stroke.

"Fuck." I toss my head back and he dips to kiss my throat, licking and sucking, grazing his teeth.

He moves in and out of me with a wicked pace, pounding my pussy like he fucking owns it.

He *does* fucking own it.

"Harder," I whisper. "Hurt me, lover."

His hand shoots up to latch around my throat, squeezing, restricting my air flow, forcing me to gasp as he thrusts into me like a maniac.

He *is* a maniac.

I'm a maniac.

We're both out of our damn minds.

His hand slips upward beneath my chin, gripping my jaw, holding my head in place as his hips work their sinful magic, stroking inside me, his cock forcing me up, up, up that peak. His eyes are darkly intent on destroying me with pleasure, holding my gaze with his power as he bites my bottom lip before sucking it into his mouth.

"Come for me."

His voice, his words, the way they stroke my soul—it ignites every particle of my being and shatters my senses, forcing me higher. Then he twists his hips as he angles up and pummels me, shoving me off the edge. I cry out as I come, and his lips on mine smother the sound. His orgasm comes with mine, linked like it was meant to be, and he growls against my mouth, the vibration of it making my lips tingle as he spills inside me.

"Do you love me?" I ask before nibbling on his lip.

He pants, taking a few heavy breaths before responding, "Love is a word and a pointless one, at that."

"Love is an action."

"Then ask me what I would do for you."

My gaze slips across his face, flickering from his eyes to his lips, and back again. "What would you do for me, lover?"

He pauses in his heavy breathing as he leans over me,

still holding my chin. He licks his lips as he looks at mine, then he kisses me with a fierce kind of tenderness.

Quiet falls between us, but I interrupt it with a rephrased question. "Would you kill for me?" I smile because I already know the answer.

His head cocks to the side as he kisses a sweet line along my jaw toward my hair. "I already have."

I swallow, moaning against the feel of his lips on my skin. "Would you die for me?"

He stills.

I sit up straighter, forcing him to straighten, too. I reach up and take his face in my hands, pulling his head down to mine, pressing our foreheads together. "Would you die for me, lover?"

"You know I would, baby doll. You know I would."

My heart thumps. I could almost cry—I won't, but I *almost* could. He kisses me sweetly, softly, a careful moment for a careful proclamation that means more to me than he could ever know.

And then the moment shatters.

We both startle as the wood door to his office splinters with a loud blow. He quickly pulls out and grabs my waist, pulling me down from the desk and shoving me behind it. He pulls his pants on as he charges toward the door being broken down. His cum is dripping down my leg as his office is being broken into, so that's fucking awesome.

The whole damn door comes down after another

forceful blow, and Castiel steps back as a group of armed men filter in.

"Shit." I crawl beneath the desk, and I'm thankful I can hide here since the desk comes all the way to the ground, completely blocking me from their sight.

Castiel shoves the desk chair in front of the opening where I hide and steps out from behind the desk, leaving my line of sight. "You could've knocked, Monroe," he says calmly, as if he knows the person who beat down his door.

"Not really my style, bro."

Bro?

It's a man's voice, deep and penetrative... familiar. It's similar to Castiel's.

"What are you doing here?"

"I'm looking for someone." The man's voice travels nearer. "A man of ours went missing a couple of days ago. We tracked his last known whereabouts to your establishment."

"Your tracking skills have taken a dive then," Castiel replies as I pull my knees tight to my chest. "Why would one of your men be here? They're not allowed. That was a part of the agreement. We check them all at the door."

But we both know one of them slipped through the cracks, got through the security protocol, and even won his bet for an hour with an angel. That man is dead, burned to ashes in the incinerator.

Castiel had to murder two of his authority who had both missed the blaringly fucking obvious, but we thought everything was managed, taken care of. I guess not since the Syndicate is now literally breaking down his damn door.

"Your security protocols must need an update then, Castiel. All our sources confirm this was his last location. But somehow, he never left the building."

The chair wheels glide along the hardwood floor as it moves backward, and I see tan combat boots appear just in front of me, olive-green camouflaged pants tucked into the top. I tense up, slowing my breaths, keeping as quiet as a mouse, hoping he won't see me.

"Where are you hiding him? Or have you already killed him? I'll have you know," he says, plopping into the desk chair and crossing an ankle over his knee, "that man was a Syndicate leader."

"I thought *you* were a Syndicate leader, Monroe. It's getting a bit difficult to keep up with all these leaders. How many men does it take to rule a city?"

"You have no idea what it takes to keep this city locked down. You have this one pitiful tower to manage, and you aren't even good enough at that to know who's coming in or going out. You weren't even aware of our presence until we broke down your door. We've already seized control of the Tower, and by association, everyone in it."

"The Tower is *mine*," Castiel growls.

The man in the chair slams his foot down and I flinch. "Not anymore. We're taking the Tower and locking it down. Everything and everyone in this building now belongs to us."

"For how long?"

"Indefinitely. If you help us sort out what happened to our man, perhaps we'll reconsider our presence."

There's a beat of silence as Monroe shifts in the chair. I subtly and quietly slide my ass against the back of the desk when he bends, his elbows landing on his knees. I gasp and cover my mouth with my hand as his face suddenly appears in front of me.

"Come on out, sweetheart. I won't bite."

Castiel's gravity tugs hard, and I feel as though it could drag me out through the back of the solid wood desk. "Leave her alone," he growls just before Monroe reaches for me.

He grabs me by my ankles and drags me forward, and I hear a sudden fight break out somewhere in the room— Castiel, no doubt. My legs twist beneath me as Monroe pulls me out, and I fall onto my back.

He gets me out from beneath the desk and drops my ankles, bending over me, preparing to pick me up from the floor, but I don't let him. I pull my knees back to my chest and thrust them forward, glad Castiel didn't remove my laced black boots before he went down on me.

I land a powerful blow against his thighs, just above his knees. He's a fucking mountain though, because all that does is cause him to stumble back a fraction of an inch. Still, it gives me enough time to scramble to my feet.

I spin and launch myself after him, even after I hear

Castiel yell for me to stop. I'm not stopping until I physically can't move anymore. I'm not bowing for the Syndicate— not this time.

Motherfuckers.

I catch him with my elbow against his jaw as I spin, and his head falls sideways. I throw a punch at his face, but his reflexes are lightning-fast. He palms my fist, stopping the blow before it can hit. His hand slips to grasp my wrist, squeezing it painfully. I throw my other fist toward his gut and it lands, but fuck, his abs are made of stone. He catches that wrist, too, bringing both of my clenched fists between us, dragging me in close.

I spit in his face.

He flinches, his eyes blinking shut. He flashes a tight smile and it makes my heart hammer, thrusting adrenaline through my veins.

This man is dangerous, I can feel it.

Not dangerous in the way Castiel is—no, this kind of dangerous scares me. He's a Syndicate leader, and these men show no mercy and give no second chances.

Though, I guess Castiel has acted the same way.

He did kill my keeper... and the two authority who fucked up and let in a Syndicate leader... *and* said Syndicate leader. So, maybe he doesn't show mercy either, but he's *mine.* He protects me and the alters, and that makes him the safest man in this Tower. It makes him the safest man in the whole fucking city for girls like me.

"Well, aren't you cute," Monroe says, shifting both of my wrists to one of his massive hands. The other finds the back of my head, grabbing me harshly and spinning me toward the desk. He wrenches my arms around behind my back before grabbing the back of my neck and slamming me down on the desk.

I don't turn my head quick enough and my nose slams into the hardwood. It sends a burst of pain through my face, disabling my sight with a moment of blackness dotted with yellow spots of starlight. When my vision returns and the pain turns to a pulsing, bruising ache, I blink open my eyes and see red—it's my own blood smeared on the desk Castiel just fucked me on.

I turn my head and let my cheek rest on the crimson as the evil man behind me presses down harshly on my neck to hold me in place. I breathe through my mouth as I wonder whether my nose is broken.

Fuck him if he did break it. I had a great fucking nose.

"Castiel," Monroe says in a goading tone, "who is this pretty little thing? I know she can't possibly be an ordinary alter. Because if she were, you wouldn't have bothered hiding her behind your desk, would you?"

I can't see Castiel, but I can hear his heavy breathing, each labored breath huffing its way out on a predatory growl. "She's no one."

"No one?" Monroe bends over me, and I feel him fold along my back. "So if I fuck her here, you'll have no problem with it?"

Shit, shit, shit.

I feel Monroe's hand creep up the back of my bare thigh, and I tense against his touch. Something resembling a whimper escapes me and I internally beg Castiel to keep quiet, to keep pretending I'm just another alter he doesn't give a shit about.

But then I realize that's impossible.

He's fucking in love with me, whether he'll admit to it with those words or not. He already killed for me once. He told me he'd die for me, and his words weren't empty.

I laugh out loud—a joyful, girly snicker—because it just hit me that the Deity is in love with me. The sound breaks through the otherwise silent room—just my laughter and heavy breathing from fighting men.

"What's so funny, fuck girl?"

"*Fuck* girl? Okay. You've got me pegged." I roll my eyes. "Go on now. Lift my skirt and sink inside me, I think you'll enjoy my pussy. But fair warning? Castiel got there first, and he's still dripping down the inside of my thigh. I don't mind a little cocktail if you want to mix in."

Monroe's fingers dig into the sides of my neck as he grips me tighter, lifts me upright off the desk, and tosses me sideways onto the floor. "Filthy fucking whore. Tie them both up and sit them over there on the couch," he demands from one of his men.

I push up onto all fours, thrusting my ass out and

turning to look over my shoulder at him, blinking against the pulsing pain in my nose. "You sure you don't want these sloppy seconds?"

"*Tempest*," Castiel says, and I whip my head around to look at him. There's a man binding his wrists with rope as he sits on the couch. My eyes squint at the disgusting sight of it.

He's the motherfucking Deity.

He's Castiel fucking King!

I don't give a shit who they are—I don't care that they're with the Syndicate—*no* one comes after Castiel, no one subdues him, no one makes him weak.

I observe Castiel carefully as someone grabs my elbow and hoists me to my feet. His lower lip is bleeding, busted open and there's blood on his knuckles. Seeing Castiel subdued, controlled, overpowered makes my stomach twist in unpleasant knots.

If they can do that to him, what will they do to the rest of us?

We were supposed to be protected here. I should be pissed at Castiel because *he* killed the Syndicate man in the White Room unknowingly. But I'm not pissed at Castiel. I'm not even pissed at the authority who fucked up their jobs and let one of the Syndicate inside the Tower to play at all.

I'm rage-filled at the Syndicate because all of this, everything I've had to endure over the last decade, is because of them, because they wanted to control the city and took it over by force. They ruined all our lives. They turned us from humanity to lives of brutality and violence—wanted or not.

Now, they want to take over my only safe-haven, the only place I've ever felt I could let my guard down in this damn city.

The Tower belongs to *us*.

And I won't let them take it.

CHAPTER TEN
possessive violence

EYES ARE ON us, like fucking hawks on mice.

Castiel and I are both bound by the wrists, sitting hip to hip on the sofa in his large office on the thirtieth floor. I rest my head on his shoulder innocently, blinking my lashes up at the guardsman watching us. I try to look as small, meek, and nonthreatening as possible. It must be working, or else these guys are fucking morons, because they don't separate us.

"Are you okay?" Castiel asks quietly, his chin nudging against my forehead as he turns his face toward mine.

"I'm fine. I think I might have a crooked nose after this, but at least I'll have a good story to tell about it." I turn my head, move my lips closer to his ear, and whisper, "We're not just going to roll over and let them take the Tower, are we?"

I pull back and catch his eyes with mine.

His eyebrows dip toward his nose and his dark eyes flicker with an expression that's absent from his face. I can't quite read the look.

"They've already taken it, baby doll, and they're not giving it back."

"So we *take* it back."

"It's not that simple."

"Don't be such a pussy."

"Shut your fucking mouth, Tempest."

"Fucking *make* me," I snarl. "I'd rather die than let them take this place from us."

His eyes lift above my head, looking behind me. "You might have to make that choice if you don't shut the fuck up."

I see movement from the corner of my eye, and my head snaps to see Monroe moving toward us. I watch him warily as he crouches to perch on the solid coffee table in front of the sofa and leans forward, clasping his hands between his spread legs with his elbows on his knees.

"What are you two lovebirds whispering about? Trying to decide who's going to tell me what happened to our man?"

I lean forward. "Even if I knew, I wouldn't tell you shit—" Castiel's bound wrists whip out in front of me, punching into my chest and shoving me backward in my seat.

"You're wasting your time." Castiel shifts, scooting forward and moving impossibly closer to me, leaning in front of me to block me with his shoulder. My stomach flutters pleasantly with the way he protects me. "Your man was never here."

"Cut the bullshit, Cas. What happened to him?"

"Are you deaf? I said he was never here."

Monroe cocks his head to the side, narrowing his eyes. "Do we need to do this the hard way?"

"Was there ever an easy way with you?"

Monroe looks at me pointedly, scanning me with his eyes, scrutinizing my appearance in a way that makes me feel naked. "She's awfully pretty… save for the broken nose."

"Yeah, thanks for that." I roll my eyes at him.

He turns his eyes to Castiel. "Does she have a death wish? Snarky little thing."

"She has no filter," Castiel replies, shifting somehow closer still.

"You like that, bro? You like a girl who talks to you like she fucking owns you? Shit, I never had you pegged for the kind of guy who'd let a bitch pussy-whip him. Does her cunt taste like honey? Is she the best you've ever fucked? Why this one?"

I turn my head to look at Castiel, waiting for his response, but it never comes. He just lets a smirk lift his cheek and the look is full of malice, contempt for the man sitting across from him.

Monroe reaches out and taps his hand roughly against Castiel's cheek, and I want to fucking slaughter him. "Come on, tell me. Why this chick?"

Castiel finally responds through gritted teeth, "I guess you'll never know."

Monroe purses his lips, nodding a little. "I guess I'll have to find out the hard way. Personally, I'm not into this snarky, punk girl attitude your girl is putting on—"

"You prefer your women meek and subservient. I know. Your fragile ego just isn't up for the challenge."

Monroe's jaw ticks, much in the same way Castiel's does when he's masking his expression.

Shit.

They look alike.

The way they seem to know each other, the hints that they're brothers, is impossible to ignore. The only thing that's different about them is the color of their hair and their eyes. Where Castiel is dark, Monroe is light—same thick, wavy hair, but Monroe's is a dirty blond and his eyes are an odd hazel shade that seems to shift constantly. But everything else is impossibly similar.

They're brothers.

Fuck, they're brothers.

Monroe stands suddenly and paces away before whipping back around to face us. "It's the hard way, then." He nods at one of the guardsman on his right. "Grab her and bend her over that desk. Gentleman, for your exhaustive efforts in honoring the Syndicate with your service, please dip your dick inside this golden honeypot pussy that has my brother so pathetically fucking whipped."

Castiel and I look at each other and something like fear flashes across his eyes. The fear in him sparks adrenaline inside me as one of the men hoists me up by the elbow and drags me across the room. I shake my head at Castiel when a rage I've never seen before threatens to mask the expressionless face I've come to love.

Love.

I shake myself from the guardsman's grip momentarily, just enough to bend to Castiel and whisper, "Don't react. I can take it, lover." I'd rather take every man in this room up the ass than see that look of fear in his eyes.

His brow creases as the guardsman yanks on my arm and pulls me away. He takes me to the desk and, just as ordered, bends me over the side of it.

God, I've spent a lot of time face-down on this desk.

He holds me down with my cheek laid against the hardwood, my tied hands squished between the desk and my chest. He grabs the back of my skirt harshly and yanks it up over my ass cheeks, exposing me to the entire room.

Do they think this will break me?

This won't break me.

But will it break Castiel?

"Is your memory jogged yet, Cas?" Monroe asks, and I can tell he's close behind me. A hand whips through the air and smacks my bare skin with a stinging *thwack*. "Are you ready to talk now?" He waits, but I don't hear a response. "Okay, then. Gentleman, who'd like to go first?"

Fuck, fuck, fuck.

I hear pants unzipping and the murmuring of male voices behind me. Every muscle in my body tenses, and I focus on my breathing. I say a quick prayer to the sex gods that my body will respond so I don't get dry fucked by a train of filthy Syndicate men.

I blink and squeeze my eyes shut, but I'm instantly taken to images of being in the city streets with my brother, being attacked, forced to suck off a bunch of assholes, only to watch my brother die. I open my eyes and keep them open. I'd rather be forced to watch this shit show happen than see my brother behind my eyes while this goes down.

Why am I letting this happen?

Fight. Run. Escape.

I want to fight. The impulse is searing through my veins with each pump of my rapidly beating heart, but something stops me.

Castiel.

The Tower.

I'm clinging to the only safety I've ever known in hopes it will be safe again.

"Stop," I hear one of the guardsman say in the distance. "Get the fuck down!"

I turn my face to look in the direction of the sound, but

everything is happening behind me. All I can see is a crowd of guards rushing toward the sofa where Castiel and I were sitting side-by-side. I hold my breath, fearful for my lover.

But I should've known I never needed to fear for Castiel…

He's a god.

He's the Deity of the Tower.

He's the one who answers my prayers and comes to my aid when I need more than I can take for myself.

Chaos erupts and there's an explosion of sound. Men grunt, fists slap, and somebody's blood sprays across the room. I flinch, pinching my eyes shut as the blood touches my cheeks, and when I open my eyes again, it's a fucking war happening behind me.

Gunfire erupts, mingling with the shouts and fighting, creating a war zone in the space behind my bare ass. I try to stand, but someone still has their hand on the middle of my back, pressing me down.

"Stay down!" he commands, but I try again.

"I'll get fucking shot!" I scream at him as bullets and blood rain all around us.

I lift again, but he pushes down.

And then suddenly, his hand is gone. I start to rise, but someone molds against me from behind, bending over me… And I know it's *him* the moment his skin touches mine.

"Time to go, baby doll."

I grin as Castiel lifts me, yanks down my skirt, and spins

me to face him. My jaw drops as I take in the sight of him. He's covered in blood from head to toe, soaked in it from the men he's slaughtered. He holds one of the guardsman's assault rifles in his grip and his chest heaves with powerful energy. His wrists are unbound, and he doesn't even appear to be injured. He just looks down at me with intense, protective energy that holds me in place.

A grin creeps across his face in possessive violence, and I feel his brutality pulse in my soul.

Fuck the Syndicate.

He quickly untangles the knots binding my wrists together before pushing me behind him. He fires off another few rounds as I rush to the nearest guardsmen on the floor and pry a handgun from his dead hand. Castiel reloads his clip as I rush back to his side.

That's when I pause and really see the mess he's made. It's a massacre. Bodies are scattered about his office, lying still on the floor. Blood pools and merges from one lifeless man to the next. A few roll and groan as they cling to life, and one crawls along the big picture window, sullying my precious view of the city I once loved.

I nod in the direction of the crawling man. "Get him, lover."

Castiel strides across the battle zone and I watch with a thumping mad heart as he lifts his boot, slams it down on the man's lower back, and forces him flat to the floor. He aims the gun at his head and fires. Blood sprays from the back of his head, covering my man with another layer of red blood and splashing across my pretty picture window.

The blood that spatters across the city view now belongs to the Syndicate, and it feels so right. They painted the streets with our blood—the blood of the innocent—and my man washed it away with theirs.

My head jerks as I see movement out of the corner of my eye. Monroe appears from behind the sofa, bloodied but alive, pointing his gun at me with an outstretched arm. He smirks as his finger covers the trigger and my dumb response is to smile, lift my hand, and wiggle my fingers at him in a goodbye, because I'm certain he's about to go down—I'm certain Castiel is about to murder him, too.

But then Castiel barrels into me, knocks me sideways to the floor with his arm around my waist just as Monroe fires his gun. The explosive sound echoes in my ears as Castiel urges me to get on all fours and we crawl for the door.

I want to scream at him, shout at him, tell him to kill Monroe and end him for good. But I can feel the last dregs of humanity and compassion for his own brother in the vibration of his soul beside me. I can feel what he feels—I don't understand it, but I can feel it.

A bullet hits the wall above our heads, splintering the wood. I flinch and let out a yelp. We scramble to our feet as we pass the threshold, and then we take off running through the black hole corridor. I punch the elevator button and we both turn with guns raised to watch the door.

"Castiel!" Monroe shouts from within.

My knees bounce, anxiously waiting for the elevator to open.

Why is there no fucking stair access out here?

"Castiel!" he calls out again. "You can't win this war!"

I open my mouth to scream back at him, but Castiel shuts me down, turning to clap a palm over my mouth. My eyes dart to his and he shakes his head as he whispers, "Don't say a word, baby doll."

I nod against his palm and the elevator dings.

The doors part just as we hear heavy footfalls padding from within the office, quickly coming toward us. We back onto the elevator with hurried steps, and I press the button to the garage level over and over again.

Tap, tap, tap, tap, tap.

I hold my breath as Monroe appears in the doorway just as the elevator doors start to slide shut. He makes a run for us, knowing Castiel already chose not to take the opportunity to murder his brother. We back up, hitting the wall, and I poise my finger over the trigger, ready to end him if he gets too close, if Castiel won't do it himself.

But just in the nick of time, the metal doors slide shut. We both exhale heavily on cue and lower our guns. We look at each other, and without missing a beat, he closes in around me, crowding me against the corner.

Looming over me, bloodied from battle, he stares at me with black hole eyes that draw me in endlessly. "Fight for you, kill for you, die for you, baby doll."

CHAPTER ELEVEN
a brutal maniac and a savior

HE KISSES ME with fury, the blood on his face smearing onto mine as he feeds me his words silently through his insistent tongue.

"Fight for you, kill for you, die for you, baby doll."

Shit, if that isn't love, then I don't know what is.

Our kiss breaks just as ferociously as it began with a snap of reason for our current predicament.

"I think we're in trouble."

He grins down at me. "Big fucking trouble."

"What do we do now?"

"We leave."

"Leave the Tower? Where will we go?"

He steps in closer, his body molding to mine and holding me firmly in the corner. "We escape the city."

My heart pounds double time. "How the hell do we do that?"

"Together." His hand comes up to stroke my hair at the side of my face, coating it crimson from his palm.

My head tilts into his hand. "I don't think I want to leave."

"Then what do you want?"

I suck my bottom lip between my teeth and give him my best puppy dog eyes. "I wanna take back the city."

It's quiet as he stares at me, impassive as ever as he silently works through what I'm telling him.

"Please, lover."

A smirk ticks up the side of his beautiful face and he steps back. He moves to the button panel and punches the button for the thirteenth floor just as we pass the fifteenth floor on the way down.

"What are you doing?"

"I'm giving you what you want, Tempest. We'll take back the city together. But we need an army."

The elevator stops on the thirteenth floor, but he hits the button to close the doors as soon as they part. There's nothing on this floor, only an unmaintained corridor of old hotel rooms from before the takeover—he just wanted to stop the elevator from going all the way down. Castiel punches the button for the twentieth floor to send the elevator back up and he gives me a knowing look.

I smile at him. "We're taking the alters?"

"And the keepers. I think they'll be happy for us to rescue them from the Syndicate invading our Tower, don't you think?"

I nod, shifting with excited energy from one foot to the other. "Let's do it."

"Stay behind me and follow my lead. The Syndicate will be on their floor, and we need to take them out as quickly as possible. Don't go shooting off rounds like a fucking maniac and risk hitting our people."

"I'm sorry… who is the fucking maniac with an assault rifle, massacring entire rooms of people?" I sarcastically tilt my head and he smirks at me. "I've got this, lover."

He moves to stand in front of me as the elevator stops on the alters' floor with a ding. I press a quick kiss on his back and whisper, "Fight for you, kill for you, die for you," and I see the way my words make him shiver.

He shows me his affection by taking a small step back, covering me more completely with his body as the metal doors open unto unknown levels of violence to come.

But we're met with silence.

I lean forward to peek around him, but then he steps forward between the elevator doors, lifting his hand to the side to catch it in case it closes on him. We both look down at the floor at the same time, and all I can see is blood.

My heart sinks.

Have they massacred the alters and keepers?

Are they already dead?

Castiel takes a careful step out of the elevator, and I rush to follow. There's a booted foot on the floor to our left, attached to a lifeless body. I scan the corpse from toe to head, and sigh a breath of relief when I see a face I don't recognize. It's not an alter or a keeper; it's a Syndicate guard, and he's dead.

Castiel and I share a puzzled look, but I think we're both filled with hope. If the guardsman at the elevator is dead and the floor is quiet, then maybe the alters and keepers are still safe, still alive.

We creep forward beneath a flickering fluorescent lightbulb overhead where a stray bullet seems to have shattered the plastic covering. There's no one in the open common area, just bloodied furniture, flickering lights, and empty space.

Castiel reaches back with one hand, guiding me behind him. We circle around the reception desk where there's normally a keeper assigned at all hours to monitor alters and to make sure no one leaves the floor without permission. But there's no one there. I cross behind Castiel and move toward the desk, peeking over the edge, expecting to see a dead keeper on the floor. But there's no dead body. I turn to look at Castiel and shrug. He looks back at me, just as puzzled.

Where are they?

"Should we check the bedrooms?" I whisper, worried we might find them all rounded up, slaughtered in one room

His shoulders slump a little and he nods. I think that's the saddest fucking thing I've ever seen him do—he's sad about the alters. As if the idea of their death actually does mean something to him, as if he really did give a shit about all of us and keeping us safe from the city from the beginning.

We're his girls.

He rescued us all and kept us safe from the Savage Syndicate. And sure, he ruled with an iron fist, but I see that he did it for our safety. Even when he killed my keeper over my social media indiscretions, he did it to ensure our future safety from the Syndicate in the Tower.

He's a brutal maniac and a savior—a truly vengeful god trying to save and protect his disciples.

I see him with new eyes, and those eyes have me falling hard, as if I hadn't already crashed and burned for this man.

"We're gonna find them," I reassure him.

His eyes flicker across my face, and I see my thoughts reflected in the darkness of his irises. He gives me a sinful grin and a wink—a fucking wink—and I think I just came. He steps closer, slinging his arm around my waist and pulling me into him. He bends and presses his lips to mine for a bruising beat. I part my lips to deepen his kiss, heart pounding because I know we're not exactly in a safe space here, but hell, is it exciting.

Then there's a crash, a metal door slamming against the wall from behind Castiel. He turns, lifts his gun, and steps in front of me to cover me. There's shouting, a female voice, then shots fired in our direction. I duck and Castiel shoves me back behind the reception counter, where I stumble to the floor.

Castiel joins me moments later, shouting at some unknown person that's shooting at us randomly. He crouches beside me and shouts, "Zola, stop!"

Silence falls.

"How do you know my name?" she shouts back.

I remember then that the alters don't know him; the keepers don't know him. He's only brought me back to my room a couple of times himself, and those were times when hardly anyone would've been around to see him. They've never met the Deity and they don't know he's on their side.

I jump to my feet, scrambling out from behind the counter, struggling against Castiel as he grabs the bottom hem of my T-shirt and tries to hold me back. He's just trying to protect me, but he doesn't need to. I know Zola, and she knows me.

I manage to get away from his pull and I jump in front of her, holding up my hands, handgun still held in one. "Zola, it's me!"

Zola is one of only a few alters on the floor that I spoke to with any sort of regularity. She's different, like me— actually, she's not like me at all, but we're both different from the other girls in our own way.

She looks at me with narrowed eyes, tossing her thick, black, braided hair behind her shoulders. Her nostrils flare over her septum piercing, and I see that her dark brown skin is spattered with blood… but I don't think it belongs to her.

"Tempest? Who is that man? Is he Syndicate?"

I shake my head, lowering my hands. "No. No, we just escaped them. Zola… he's the *Deity*."

"The—" She cocks her head to the side. "The Deity? He's alive?"

My brow furrows. "Yes, he's alive. They tried to take us, but we may have left a bit of a bloody mess upstairs. Where is everyone?"

Castiel slips out from behind the counter then, slowly, warily, and Zola still has her gun raised, ready to fire at him.

She jerks her head back toward the door she came bursting through, scrutinizing Castiel with narrowed eyes. "In the stairwell. But we can't access the garage level to get out. Are you really the Deity?"

"Yes," Castiel replies. "Your keepers should be able to open the door with retinal scans."

Zola shakes her head, finally lowering her gun. "It's not working."

Castiel huffs out a frustrated groan. "They must have disabled stairwell access before they took over."

"Can you get us out of here?" she asks.

"The gambling floor on the main level runs on a different access system, so we might be able to get out there. But it will be swarming with Syndicate… especially once word gets out about what I did upstairs."

"Your brother has probably already called in back-up," I say.

"Your brother?" Zola asks.

"Girl, there is so much happening here that you don't know about. And I will tell you all about it later. But right now, we need to get the fuck out of here. They're gonna kill us all if we don't."

"How many of you survived?" Castiel asks.

"All of us," Zola says with a shrug.

I look at Castiel. "That's fifteen alters, fifteen keepers, you and I included. We can still outnumber them if we move fast… if we get out before their back-up arrives. Burn down the fucking building behind us."

Castiel pauses, taking in the information, and I can see wheels turning behind his eyes. Then he nods, looking at Zola. "Are you all armed?"

"Just a few of us, with the guns we took from the Syndicate we killed. The keepers couldn't get access to the weapons storage room, either."

"Fuck. Okay. Call them all back in here. Have them find whatever they can use as a weapon… fucking butter knifes and staplers if that's all they can find."

Zola's eyes widen. "You want *me* to tell them?"

"You seem to be leading this operation well enough on your own. Round up your troops, soldier."

Zola is too fucking cute with the way a devious smirk creeps up the side of her cheek. She gives a single nod.

"Okay, then."

We share a look and I smile at her broadly, bouncing in place with anxiety and a strange sort of excitement for the battle ahead. I would probably be clapping if I didn't have a gun in hand.

I turn to Castiel and press my body to his, pushing him back to the counter. "We can do it," I tell him excitedly as alters and keepers start to filter back onto the floor from the stairwell. I can feel their eyes on us—well, I can feel their eyes watching Castiel, regarding the Deity with awe and confusion.

And he's my fucking man.

He bends, snaking his hand to the back of my neck to hold me in place as he kisses me with lips and tongue and teeth. "I fucking love you," he says, and all the air inside my lungs leaves me with a single exhale.

"I fucking love you, Cas. Don't die, okay? It'll really hurt my feelings if you kick the bucket without me." I smile.

"Gods never die, baby doll. And I'm not letting anything happen to you, either."

CASTIEL AND I creep toward the metal door in the stairwell once we've all descended to the main level—the gambling floor. It's deadly silent as we press our ears to the door with no window to peek through. It should be noisy with voices and music, but it isn't. It's silent, and that's fucking eerie.

We share a glance with each other, then Castiel turns to the group behind us.

"We need to be quick. Straight across the gambling floor is the main entrance. That's our exit. We make it there and we run for it. The Syndicate will show you no mercy, so show them none in return. Escaping is the priority, but if you must fight, fight to kill."

"We're demons tonight, ladies. Kill or be killed," I add.

Castiel nods at me and moves toward the retinal scanner on the wall beside the door. He stands in front of it and holds still as the red beam of light makes the scan. It beeps once and we hear the internal lock click, indicating that the door is open. I think we all sigh a collective breath of relief that it worked, but the relief is short-lived, immediately followed by a chorus of sharp inhales in preparation for the battle to come.

Castiel grabs the metal handle on the door and pulls— just enough to keep it from locking again—and gives a final glance back at our crew of thirty.

Surely, they can't kill us all…

I don't want them to kill a single one of us. I'm not exactly popular and I never really did take the chance to get to know all the other alters, but in a strange sort of way, these people are the only family I've got. We've all been wrecked and ruined in the same ways at the hand of the Savage Syndicate, and that shared trauma creates an unbreakable bond. I don't have to know them individually to care about them, and I think Castiel feels the same.

He and I share a look and a nod before he wrenches open the door and charges through it. I follow behind and the others file through after us. Five paces forward and we all come to a stop, the alters and keepers fanning out in the space behind me and Castiel.

The gambling floor is a vast, open space with a concrete floor, only broken up by the eight floor-to-ceiling circular cages that line the aisleway—which runs straight down the middle—with four cages on each side. Players place bets on the fighters in those cages.

But the floor is silent.

Purple neon and black lights flicker and falter around the space, casting a creepy dark light over the dead bodies on the floor. Fighters in cages, players surrounding, several dozen dead, their blood pooling in black puddles and spatters under the dim lighting.

I turn to Castiel and find that he's already looking at me, the whites of his eyes casting a silver glow around his blackened irises. His hand reaches out toward me, and I put my palm in his. He squeezes, making my heart flutter. The adrenaline already pumping through my veins kicks up a notch at his touch. We creep forward with care.

I'm hypervigilant—I think we all are—as we move down the center aisle. My eyes dart rapidly, searching for movement, any signs of an oncoming attack.

We pass the first set of two cages, one on each side of

us. We pass the second set, and I'm starting to feel hopeful. But the hope is tinged with a nagging feeling that it can't possibly be this easy. There's no way we'll be able to just walk out of here without a fight—no fucking way.

The exit is in sight as we approach the end of the third set of cages. Down a quick dash of two open staircases, we'll find the door that leads outside, opening onto the city streets.

"Help..." a strangled groan whispers from a bleeding man on the floor, just beyond the end of the third set of cages. "They're... they..."

The dying man struggles to get our attention and I hesitate, watching his eyes and how they flicker from us to the corridor behind him. It opens up just at the start of the fourth set of cages—an offset space with a bar and stations for the bookies where players officially place their bets.

Castiel is already wary of the space as we approach, tugging on my hand to guide me behind him. We keep moving, slowly, our guards up and ready to take on the fight.

But no one can ever really be prepared for a war.

With no warning, the flashing lights of gunfire suddenly brighten the dim space as a dozen or more men appear from that offset corridor, igniting the stale air with their weapons, threatening to end us all with the exit in sight.

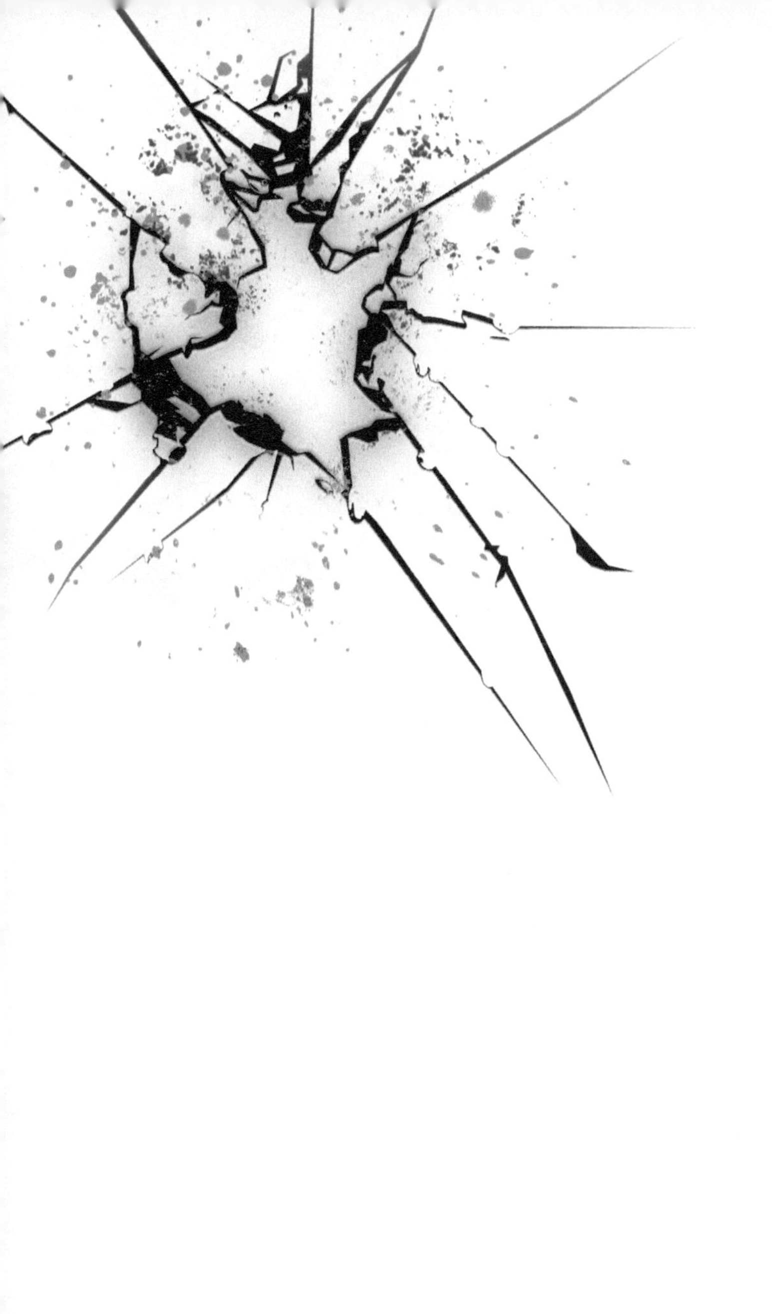

CHAPTER TWELVE
endgame

CASTIEL REACHES OUT to shove me down out of the line of
fire, but I'm already crouching toward the floor, scrambling
quickly along the side of the cage closest to the gunfire and
around behind it as the alters and keepers scatter. I know
I'm too proud and brave for my own good in this moment,
because my instinct is to chase after the violence and meet
it with violence of my own.

"Tempest, *run!*" I hear Castiel scream at me. "Get out
of the building!"

He's smart, he's right, I should be fleeing toward the
exit. But instead, I'm running toward the corridor that
opens off to our right, the place from which I see the armed
men moving forward from and onto the gambling floor...
coming after my people. I stay slightly behind the metal

fencing that forms the cage, edging around it and looking for the best point of attack.

A Syndicate shooter sees me and turns in my direction, sending off a flurry of rounds from his automatic gun. I duck, instinctively cover my head with my free hand, but he doesn't scare me. I aim for his bulky thigh, a spot that isn't covered in armor, and shoot. The bullet strikes him, slicing into his flesh as blood bursts from the spot. He screams and drops to his knees before tumbling to the floor.

Castiel comes out from nowhere, charging forward from behind me and shooting the guy in the head, making sure he doesn't get up from the floor again. He rapid fires and takes out three more Syndicate guards coming in this direction without batting an eye.

How does he fucking do that?

Sex god and war god all in one.

I see the chaos erupting around the gambling floor. The guards rushing in, taking out alters and keepers left and right. My eyes widen, seeing them drop like flies, one after the other after the other.

"Baby, let's *go*!" Castiel shouts as he grabs my elbow, hoisting me up from my haunches.

He drags me forward as I look behind me, horrorstruck at the way the Syndicate is once again taking everything from me. I glance at Castiel and the fear in his eyes is real—and it's not even fear for himself. It's fear for *me*; it's fear for the alters and keepers.

There's a silent moment where the whole world slows down and I can't even hear what he's screaming at me as he forces me to run with him, as my legs move beneath me without my conscious thought. We have the guards outnumbered, but they have us out-weaponed.

It's never been clearer than it is at this very moment that there is no hope for the Tower—there was never a choice for us to stay or go once the Syndicate came in looking for their man. There's no hope that this place will ever be safe again. I didn't realize how this place had become my home until I was forced to leave it.

I can't stay.

But I also can't let them take it.

I shake my arm from Castiel's grip and dodge right, sprinting off toward the bar once all the Syndicate guards appear to have moved onto the floor to go after the others.

"Tempest!" Castiel shouts, and I can sense him running after me.

I leap for the countertop at the bar, climb up, sit my ass on it, spin and jump down on the other side. Castiel turns to fire off a few rounds and takes out another guard before he follows my lead, leaping behind the bar with me. I'm already searching as his hand finds my hair, gripping it at the base of my neck and tugging me backward to a stop.

"What the fuck are you doing?"

"Let go! I need to find a lighter."

"A lighter? For what?"

I pause, and though it's probably only a half a second that I stare at him, it feels like longer. "I'm burning this bitch to the ground."

His eyes narrow at me. "What?"

"If we can't have the Tower, then *they* can't have the Tower. It's *ours*, Castiel. Ours! Now help me find a lighter!"

I pull open cabinet doors, searching, and it feels like it takes him forever to get on board with me, though it's probably only seconds. I hear him huff as he spins around, reaching up onto the shelves behind the bar, trying to find one.

"Found it," I shout over gunfire as I reach for the blue lighter on a shelf beside the sink.

I set my gun and the lighter on the counter, then grab and open a bottle of vodka before setting that down, too. I grab a corkscrew and use the pointed metal tip of the spiral to puncture the bottom of my T-shirt and drag it across the fabric, creating a tear. I set the corkscrew down beside the bottle of vodka and grab the torn fabric, pulling and ripping it all the way around my body, taking off a nice chunk of material for the Molotov cocktail I'm trying to make—and making a rather cute crop top in the process, if I do say so myself.

I haphazardly dump vodka all over the wadded-up fabric in my hand, soaking it completely. I take a quick swig because, fuck, I need a drink, and stuff the soaked fabric into the bottle. I glance up at Castiel, who picks up the lighter before I can reach for it.

"Let's go," he says, and I follow him out around the side of the bar. We jog forward a few paces and he hands me the lighter just before he turns and shoots behind us. He yells at Zola and a few other girls who paused to see what we're doing. "Get out! Go!"

I spark a flame, set the rag on fire, and hurtle the bottle, aiming for the shelves of liquor on the back wall. It smashes into a row of bottles and shatters in a flash fire that makes us both jump back. The flames lick bright orange and grow quickly, burning hotter and faster from the fumes of vapor that leach from the broken bottles of liquor.

I'm entranced by the flames, empowered by them, knowing they mean I've taken back control.

I'm not playing by the Syndicate's rules anymore. I'm not dropping to my knees and taking their bullshit anymore. I'm burning down my own home just to make a point, and I'll burn the whole damn city just to show them who exactly they're fucking with.

And I won't have to do it alone.

I reach for Castiel's hand and find he's already reaching for mine. Hand in hand, we sprint for the exit. We rush down the first flight of stairs and three guards follow after us—our numbers are down by half, but half is better than nothing. We reach the landing after the first set of stairs and the guards are right on us.

"Watch out!" Zola shouts, popping up from halfway

down the next staircase.

They all stopped to give us cover... They stopped and waited for us to give us cover.

That's fucking family right there.

I duck and Castiel's arm wraps around my waist as he bends over me, letting the others fire off their remaining rounds at the three guards behind us. As Castiel and I run off to the right along the landing, bent over to avoid the gunfire, one of the guards appears in front of us. He's unarmed, but as we both jerk upright, he takes a swing at me.

I lean right and his fist flies right on past me, but Castiel doesn't miss a beat. He swoops in with the butt of his rifle to thwack the guy across the jaw, sending him flying down the second staircase.

Flames fly, heat pulses, and a thunderous *boom* rings in my ears as a small explosion kicks up behind the bar. Everyone flinches away from it.

"Let's go!" I shout and turn toward the staircase.

Before I can run for it, Castiel lassoes his arm around my waist from the side, pulls me in close to his hip, and lifts me from the ground with his superhuman strength... *God-like* strength.

My lover is a fucking god.

He trudges down the second staircase with heavy footfalls, gripping me tightly so his hand feels like it's bruising against my stomach. I throw my arms around his neck and hold tight, lifting my weight to make it easier for him to carry me. I'm not gonna deny him the pleasure of taking me to safety. It's just the gravity between us, anyway—always insisting that we get closer by any means necessary.

The others get to the bottom of the staircase first, shoving open the doors and running out onto the city streets. Just before the landing, I see movement from the other side of Castiel. One last Syndicate guard. I push off from Castiel, jump down the last two steps to the landing in front of him, aim my gun, and pull the trigger.

Pop, pop.

He lands on the marbled floor with a thud just before Castiel hits the landing beside me.

"Nice shot, baby doll." He steps forward and pushes the door open for me.

I step through with a grin. "Thank you, lover."

And just like that, we're back on the city streets—back to where we came from, back to where we never thought we'd have to return. But it doesn't feel so hopeless to be out here now. It's actually quiet on the sidewalk. The gunfire has ceased and night has fallen. It's empty, quiet, an abandoned, bloody city whose streets I haven't walked at night in a long damn time.

And for once, I'm not walking them alone.

I hop off the sidewalk as the surviving alters and keepers cheer for our escape, watching the orange flames flicker as they spread across the gambling floor, dark black smoke collecting and billowing down the staircases just inside the doors.

I back up into the center of the street, stretching my arms wide as I look up at the Tower from the outside. My eyes keep going, up, up, up, to the top of the building and beyond, staring up at the dark sky and marveling at the fact that I can actually see the stars. The city is so dim now that they shine so much brighter.

I take in a deep breath, inhaling the wafting scent of hellfire as it burns from within. Castiel smells sinfully like hellfire, too—flames burn bright within him, his strangling smolder of fire and smoke seeping in through my pores. He wraps his arms around me as he comes up behind me, spreading his legs wide and sinking so he can place his chin on my shoulder.

"You're full of surprises, baby doll."

I grin, turning my face toward him. "You like it."

"I fucking love it."

"So, what now?"

"You wanted to take back the city."

"Yeah."

"So, we take back the damn city."

I whip around to face him in a flash, grabbing his cheeks in my filthy, bloody hands. "But first, we dance." I smack his lips with a quick kiss, grab his hand, and lift it up for me to duck beneath and do a little twirl. I spin out away from him, and he tugs on my hand to whip me back in.

"You're a beautiful fucking psycho, you know that?"

I nod. "And I'm all yours."

"All mine."

I take Castiel's hand, and we run away with our small surviving crew. There's no plan or place for us; we just know we need to run to survive. We don't stop for a mile, ducking into an alleyway to catch our breath and collectively regroup. As the others crouch and sit to rest, Castiel pushes me against a brick wall deeper within the alley, hidden away in shadows.

His lips find my neck and he smothers me with affection, heating me from the inside out with his mouth teasing along the curve of my neck. My hands find his chest, gripping his T-shirt in my fists to hold him against me as my body curves to his. His mouth brushes over the shell of my ear and he whispers the only words I need to hear to know that he's mine, that he's claimed me, that I'm his forever—no matter what happens next.

"Fight for you, kill for you, die for you, baby doll."

He kisses me and it hits me like a magnetic field whipping around us, lassoing us together infinitely. Our gravity centers merge as our tongues swirl. We find our purpose within the madness in this twisted, violent world that the Savage Syndicate has created.

Separate, we were limited.

But together, he and I could rule.

Maybe it will take weeks, months, years before we take

back the city for those it belongs to. But however long it takes, we'll be together, fighting those vicious men with the same kind of brutality they bred within us.

Castiel and I are endgame.

And the Syndicate's reign ends with us.

CONNECT WITH BRYNN

Website
brynnford.com

Goodreads
goodreads.com/brynnfordauthor

BookBub
bookbub.com/profile/brynn-ford

Instagram
@brynnfordauthor
instagram.com/brynnfordauthor

TikTok
@brynnfordauthor
tiktok.com/@brynnfordauthor

Facebook Page
facebook.com/brynnfordauthor

Brynn's Daring Darlings
(Facebook Group)
bit.ly/brynnsdarlings

BRYNN'S BOOKS

THE FOUR FAMILIES TRILOGY
Counts of Eight
Dance with Death
Pas de Trois

THE FOUR FAMILIES SPIN-OFF
King of Masters

EMBER GLEN
Spark of Madness
Blaze of Misery
Embers of Mercy

SENSELESS
Unheard
Unseen

LAWLESS
Coming Soon!
The Darkness We Hide

STANDALONES
Jagged Line Paradise
Sugar Wood
The Alter

ABOUT THE AUTHOR

Brynn Ford is a USA Today Bestselling Author of dark romance for daring readers. She writes emotionally heavy love stories that will twist your soul and shatter your heart before pulling you back together with a hopeful happily-ever-after.

Brynn's books are dark, sometimes disturbing, and often overwhelming. But they're always brightened by an insistent, spicy romance that will live rent-free in your head long after you've turned the final page.

When Brynn isn't obsessively writing, you may find her binge-watching favorite shows while eating far too much junk food or fanatically reading, always seeking to lose herself in the emotional roller coaster of a damn good story. She's a firm believer that her characters continue to live outside the pages in the minds of her readers. Stories don't end just because there aren't any more pages to turn.